W9-BFG-311

JUST A MATTER OF TIME

Burning with curiosity, Rachel moved a few feet down the hedge and peeked through the tangle of vines and leaves. What she saw made her eyes go wide and pulled a soft gasp from her throat.

It was the captain. The man was bathing, naked, in the pond.

He had a rich golden tan all over his body, and the sight of him created a heavy, warm sensation in the pit of Rachel's belly. She wondered what he'd do if he looked up and discovered her watching him, and the very idea made her heart pound even more.

Then he started walking toward her. . . .

Books by Suzanne Elizabeth

When Destiny Calls
Fan the Flame
Kiley's Storm
Destined to Love
Destiny Awaits
Till the End of Time
*Destiny's Embrace**

Published by HarperPaperbacks

*coming soon

Till the End of Time

⋄ SUZANNE ELIZABETH ⋄

HarperPaperbacks
A Division of HarperCollins*Publishers*

If you purchased this book without a cover, you should be aware that this book is stolen property. It was reported as "unsold and destroyed" to the publisher and neither the author nor the publisher has received any payment for this "stripped book."

This is a work of fiction. The characters, incidents, and dialogues are products of the author's imagination and are not to be construed as real. Any resemblance to actual events or persons, living or dead, is entirely coincidental.

HarperPaperbacks   *A Division of* HarperCollins*Publishers*
10 East 53rd Street, New York, N.Y. 10022

Copyright © 1995 by Suzanne E. Witter
All rights reserved. No part of this book may be used or reproduced in any manner whatsoever without written permission of the publisher, except in the case of brief quotations embodied in critical articles and reviews. For information address HarperCollins*Publishers*,
10 East 53rd Street, New York, N.Y. 10022.

Cover illustration by Pino Daeni

First printing: November 1995

Printed in the United States of America

HarperPaperbacks, HarperMonogram, and colophon are trademarks of HarperCollins*Publishers*

❖ 10 9 8 7 6 5 4 3 2 1

I'm told that every now and then in a writer's life a really stubborn book comes along, one that takes a little more hard work and determination than usual. For many different reasons this was such a book for me. And with this in mind, I would like to thank my friends and family for putting up with my long absence, both physical and mental. I'd also like to thank my editor for allowing me the time I needed to make Scott and Rachel's story as special as I could. And thank you to my readers, who take time out of their own busy schedules to write me warm letters of encouragement.

This one is for all of you.

Till the End of Time

1

Seattle, Washington 2001

Considering he'd recently acquired the power to manipulate time, Scott Ramsey figured it was pretty ironic that he was running twenty minutes late.

He scooped up the black and white cat edging perilously close to the hot coffeepot and dropped him down onto the floor while popping the last of a toasted English muffin into his mouth. He downed the rest of his black coffee, snatched his car keys off the countertop, and turned to find Rowdy, a fat, cantankerous tabby, mauling his black canvas duffle bag.

"Aw hell. Get away from there!"

The cat did a half-gainer followed by a backward somersault and tore off into the living room. Scott reached for his bag. "You're due for stew, kitty cat," he warned.

"I catch you sizing that fella up for a pot, and he won't be the only one floating around among sliced potatoes and peas."

Scott looked up to see his grandmother shuffling into the kitchen wearing her yellow quilted robe and floppy white slippers. Despite the heated argument they'd had the night before, he managed a tight smile. "Good morning, Grandma."

"He plays with your things because he likes you so much," she said, heading for the counter.

Scott examined the frayed nylon handle of his duffle bag. "Thank God he doesn't *hate* me." But the minor bites and scratches on the bag were nothing compared to the declining condition of his running shoes. No matter where Scott hid them, that damn cat always seemed to nose out his expensive Nikes.

"Why are you still here?" his grandmother asked, pouring herself a cup of coffee. "It's almost eight-thirty."

Scott eyed the crafty, ninety-three-year-old woman. "I overslept."

"I told you you paid too much for that alarm clock."

"Somebody snuck into my room last night and turned it off."

"Really?" she replied innocently.

"And I doubt it was one of the cats."

"Oh, I don't know," she said, turning toward him. "Cleo turned the television set on just the other day."

Scott tucked his bulky duffle bag under his arm. "I think human sabotage is definitely afoot."

"Are you implying that *I* turned it off?" Her wrinkled eyes widened. "*Me*? A poor, defenseless old woman who isn't even capable of living on her own, much less operating a complicated device such as an alarm clock?"

"Grandma," Scott said patiently. "We decided this issue last night."

"No, *you* decided this issue last night."

"I looked over the brochures and gave you my answer. It's not a good idea."

"And who died and made you the boss?"

"Grandfather," he replied.

"Bah." She sipped her coffee. "He was an old fool leaving you in charge of all my money."

"He was only trying to make things easier on you. At the risk of *my* sanity," he added dryly.

"Well, living with *you* this past year has certainly been no picnic. Put yourself in my place for a moment and imagine how you'd feel taking orders from someone who used to get a kick out of tinkling on your rosebushes."

Scott broke into a smile. She had a point. "I'm just trying to look out for your best interests."

"I am not a child, Scott Jacob Ramsey."

"Turning off my alarm clock because you lost an argument isn't exactly mature, Grandma."

"Neither is watching Saturday morning cartoons, but you still do that."

Scott let out a long sigh, wondering if this issue was ever going to be dropped. "Grandma, I made this decision with your best interests at heart. What if something happened to you in that place and there was nobody there to help?"

"I will have a roommate," she replied imperiously, as if that solved everything.

"Patricia Hollenbeck is ninety-five years old, weighs eighty pounds—if she weighs an ounce—and has arthritis in every joint of her body. I highly doubt she'd be effective in an emergency."

"There's an emergency call button in every room, Scotty, and always someone in the front office."

"*Strangers*, Grandma. You'd be looked after by

strangers. How would I know they're treating you with dignity and respect?"

"You mean as opposed to how you treat me here?" she replied with a martyred glimmer in her faded blue eyes.

Scott stared at her for a moment, and then smiled and shook his head. His grandmother had always been a free spirit, and he could understand why this meant so much to her. But he'd promised his dying grandfather that he'd look after her—and all six of her cats—in her final years, and he wasn't going to back out on the obligation now just because she'd gotten a wild hair about moving out on her own. "My answer is still no."

"Bah," she said, waving her hand at him. "You're as stubborn as your grandfather was." She shuffled back toward her bedroom with her coffee. "Someday you're going to find yourself a wife to lord over. I just hope that day comes before I'm moldering in a cold, dark grave."

"Don't hold your breath," Scott grumbled without thinking.

She turned back to give him a narrow-eyed stare. "What's wrong with you anyway? How come you don't have a steady girlfriend to occupy your free time?"

"Because I'm too busy placating my dear old grandmother," he said playfully.

But they both knew there was more to the matter than that. Scott was pushing thirty, and everyone he knew was married—or had at least played the matrimonial game once. But he was still standing on the sidelines, waving all the eligible women past him while waiting for that one magical lady to come along.

His friends all said he was crazy, that the perfect woman didn't exist, and that eventually he was going to have to settle for adequate. But Scott wasn't a settling kind of guy. As far as he was concerned, if the perfect woman for him didn't exist, then he'd be single for the rest of his life. In the meantime, he had his hands full with his cantankerous grandmother.

He checked his wristwatch. "Christ, I've gotta get going." He grabbed another English muffin from the open bag on the counter.

"You running another of those *mysterious* tests today?"

"Yeah. But I'll be home in time to make supper."

"Bring home burgers. With extra—"

"Extra pickles, I know. You oughta lay off those things. They could be the reason you're such an old sourpuss."

She gave him a blank stare. "Aren't you lucky, Scotty. It seems you've inherited your grandfather's remarkable sense of humor as well."

"See you later, Grandma," he said as he headed through the living room toward the front door. "And I suggest you keep Rowdy out of my bedroom. The next time I catch him makin' love to my Nikes, I'm gonna make a hat out of his furry little butt."

"Captain Ramsey, you're exactly thirty-seven minutes late."

Scott looked up from the security officer seated at Hangar 23's identification desk and smiled at Colonel Roger Tayback, the officer in charge of Project Stargazer. "I had a slight problem waking up this morning, Colonel."

"Get a fur ball stuck in your alarm?" the man asked, his lips twitching. The colonel was well aware of Scott's living situation.

"Not exactly. My grandmother is now resorting to terrorist tactics to get her way."

The colonel smiled broadly. "That Heloise is quite a card."

"Yep. Quite a card . . ."

"Ah, Captain," the colonel said, stepping forward to throw an arm over Scott's shoulders. "As my mother always said, 'Enjoy 'em now, 'cause things'll only get worse as they get older.'"

"I think she was probably referring to children, sir."

"Hell, that's true," the man said with a boisterous laugh. "And if Heloise gets any older we'll have to get a burning permit to light her birthday candles. But I'm sure my sainted mother's advice works even in this situation, Captain. You gotta be firm," he said, clenching his fist. "Set limits. Let 'em know who's boss from the get-go."

Scott nodded, although he was having a hard time visualizing his grandmother allowing him to limit her on anything.

"Try takin' television away. It always worked on Roger Junior."

"Cruel and unusual punishment, sir," Scott replied. "One night without Wheel of Fortune and the woman would crack."

"Likes that show does she?"

"Likes it? When the People's Choice survey comes out in *TV Guide*, my grandmother writes in Pat Sajak as her favorite dramatic actor."

The colonel laughed and stepped away. "Like I said, that woman is quite a card. You ready for today's transport?"

"I'm looking *forward* to some time away."

"Good. Good. 'Cause I hear it's gonna be a doozy."

Scott gave the man a steady look. "I'm not going to get my eyebrows singed off again, am I?"

"That little problem's been completely corrected with the addition of the coolers. And that nasty bout with the tree has been corrected with the implementation of an advanced directional device. Don't you worry about a thing."

"And that little *thing* about me being stranded without an oar on the last mission?"

The colonel smiled. "All taken care of. You see how this is working, Captain? You help us find the glitches, and we make sure you go down in the history books."

"Well here's hoping I don't have to disintegrate before you find your next big glitch."

The colonel was still grinning when Pete Averies, one of the computer engineers on Project Stargazer, walked up to them. "Hello, gentlemen. Scott, you hear the big news?"

"I was just about to tell him," the colonel replied. He stole a glance at his watch. "But I'll leave that honor to you, Averies. I'll see you in five, Captain."

"So what's the news?" Scott asked Pete as the colonel walked away. "The big guy seems downright perky today."

Pete, barely containing a smile, rocked back on his heels. "They're planning to attempt a future shoot next month."

"You're kidding. I thought they'd determined it implausible."

"Judging by the information you've been bringing back they're starting to think it might be worth a shot."

"Worth a shot to *them*. Who's the poor guy they're going to send?"

Pete grinned. "You."

"*Me?* Well, don't I feel blessed."

"Ah, everybody knows the entire success of this project can be laid at your feet, Scotty boy. You may not have invented the technology for Stargazer, but if it hadn't been for you, the know-how would have been worthless. Nobody else had the balls to actually step into that chamber. Nobody"—Pete poked him in the chest—"but you."

Nice sentiment, Scott thought, but he wasn't so sure courage had anything to do with it. It was probably glory-seeking stupidity that had brought him to this point. "You're not gonna get weepy on me, are you, Pete?"

"The guys and I *were* thinking about getting you a nice card."

"Captain Ramsey," a sexy female voice said over the intercom system. "Please report to the transportation lab. . . . Captain Scott Ramsey."

Both Scott and Pete glanced up at the speakers high above their heads. "Man," Pete said. "I gotta meet that woman."

"She probably *looks* like the bad side of a hyena."

"With a voice like that, I can always close my eyes and *feel* my way around."

"Hey, where's the game tonight?" Pete asked as the two of them headed toward the second-floor stairs.

"Joe's. And you better be there. You're into me for thirty bucks."

"Uh-huh, and if I recall correctly, you're into your sweet old grandmother for twenty-five."

Scott laughed. "She told me to keep it. Says I should use it to buy myself a decent haircut."

"You know, I gotta hand it to you, Scott. Having my grandmother around all the time would drive me stark raving mad."

"I'm not as sane as I look, Pete. She actually came to me last night with brochures for Oak Haven. She's gotten it into her head to move in there with a friend of hers."

"Oak Haven? Isn't that a retirement community?"

"I hear some of those places treat their residents pretty lousy."

"Oak Haven's supposed to be a pretty nice place. Wouldn't mind checkin' it out myself in another sixty years."

Scott grunted. "I can see it now. You, hobbling along, chasing after little old ladies with your oxygen tank dragging behind you."

"So, are you going to let her go?"

"My grandmother doesn't need Oak Haven. She's got me."

"That's awfully decent of you, Scotty boy, but has it ever occurred to you that *you* might not be so great? I mean, we're not talking about living with one of the guys, here, we're talking about a ninety-year-old woman who doesn't exactly share your same interests. Hell, you don't know the first thing about playing shuffleboard."

"So you're saying I should trust her care to some orderly armed with a bottle of sedatives and an enema tube?"

"If that's what she wants."

"I don't think she knows what she wants. That's why I was left in charge."

Pete paused and turned to him at the bottom of the steps. "So you told her no?"

"Of course I told her no."

Pete broke into laughter. "Welcome to granny hell, my friend."

"Thanks, Pete," Scott said dryly as he headed up the stairs. "I always appreciate your support."

"See you later today!" Pete called after him. "And bring cash to the game! I'm feeling lucky—and I don't take checks!"

Scott gave him a quick wave before turning down the long hallway toward the transportation lab.

"Three minutes before liftoff," Colonel Tayback called to him from the lab's doorway. "Let's move it along, Captain."

The usual three scientists were waiting for Scott in the lab to run the usual last-minute tests. They swarmed around him in their white lab coats, their expressions tense with concentration. To date, Scott had never seen any of them laugh, and he was on a constant mission to get one of them to crack a smile.

As his vital signs were being checked, he turned to one of them and said, "Hey, Girney. What do you have when you've got two little green balls in your hand?" Doctor John Girney didn't respond.

"Kermit the Frog's undivided attention."

The man didn't even flinch, and Scott began to wonder if a sense of humor was something they extracted in exchange for a Ph.D. "Everything's stable," Girney said to the other two with him.

"All right, Captain," Tayback said. "Let's make this one pristine. Dr. Girney, would you like to explain things to our test pilot?"

The tall, Nordic-looking man nodded. "Our target today is Georgia, 1862."

"The Civil War," Scott replied.

The colonel leaned close enough to whisper, "That's where the dart landed this morning."

Girney handed Scott a gray satchel. "Put this in your duffle bag. Inside is everything you'll need for your tests this afternoon. Now, remember," he added, "the first thing you do when you arrive is observe your physical condition."

"If I so much as burp I'll be sure to take note of the moment," Scott replied as he unzipped his duffle bag and pushed the satchel down inside.

"When you arrive, write down any and all observations," Girney continued without missing a beat, "no matter how insignificant they might seem to you. Do you have any questions?"

"Yeah," Scott said. He looked up and gave the man a serious stare. "Do you guys want a stool sample this time?"

There was a moment of utter silence in the room, and then the colonel broke into laughter. "He's kiddin', fellas. He's just kiddin'. Holy Christ, you boys really need to invent yourselves some sense of humor."

Scott and the colonel were still chuckling as they followed Dr. John Girney to the transportation cubicle. "We've corrected the high-intensity noise you've been experiencing," Girney said.

Scott pulled the foam earplugs out of the front pocket of his jeans and tossed them to the colonel. "Guess I won't need these anymore then."

"And we've strengthened the portal," Girney added. "It should come back for you in exactly six hours without a hitch." He pushed a button and the chamber door slowly swung open, releasing a frigid blast of air that hit Scott full in the face.

"And if it doesn't come back for me!" Scott shouted above the roaring of the coolers.

"Then sit tight like you did the last time!" the colonel replied. "We won't strand you there, son!"

Scott nodded, hoping that promise wouldn't have to be tested again. He hadn't exactly enjoyed his overextended stay in the open wilderness of 1921 Colorado.

"Godspeed, Captain!" the colonel shouted. "We all have every confidence that you will make this mission as successful as the rest!"

"See you at 1800 hours!" Scott shouted back.

And then, wearing nothing to protect him against the cold but a long-sleeved shirt and a faded pair of jeans, Scott stepped down three metal steps and into the transportation cubicle for Project Stargazer's fourth mission.

The heavy metal door swung shut behind him, sealing him in, and he walked to the center of the brilliantly lit, cylindrical room. Now it was up to him to step through the computer-generated time-portal.

It was times like this when Scott felt like a pig being led to slaughter. He was certainly taking a big risk every time he strolled through this door. But he wouldn't die, he couldn't. His grandmother would never forgive him if he did.

In fact, she'd probably bury him in the backyard just so she could berate him every morning over coffee.

He took a tighter grip on the handle of his duffle bag and, feeling the adrenaline begin to pump through his veins, walked forward. A strong magnetic pull began to affect his body. His skin started to tingle. A feeling of exhilaration overcame him, and all the air was forced out of his lungs. Then, in the blink of an eye, his heart stopped beating and his mind went blank. In that instant Scott Ramsey was pulled away in a cloud of atoms and scattered through time like dust on the wind.

2

Glennville, Georgia 1862

The empty china teacup toppled from Rachel
Ann Warren's knee and bounced on the Oriental rug at
her feet. Considering all the work she'd been doing on
her manners lately, Rachel knew she should have been
embarrassed by such clumsiness. But the accident was
minor compared to what her aunt had just said to her.

"Good heavens, Rachel Ann, do be careful," her
Aunt Penelope chastised. "That china is almost a century old."

"I'm sorry, Auntie," Rachel said, bending down to
retrieve the delicate cup. "You said you'd like me to
what?"

"I realize that this is rather sudden, considering you've
only been with us for two weeks, but a lady must always
be aware of her future. Tell me you'll at least consider
the idea, my dear." The woman smiled. "Beauregard
Bodain would make an excellent husband."

Then why don't you marry him, Rachel thought muti-nously. Rumor had it Beau Bodain had refused to join the war effort because he was afraid the powder residue in the air after battle would damage his skin.

Penelope Clayborn sat quietly across from Rachel in a green velvet Queen Anne chair, her rose-colored grena-dine dress looking perfect, her ebony hair only faintly streaked with gray and coiled immaculately upon her head. Her hands were folded in her lap—very cor-rectly—and she was waiting with proper Southern patience for her niece to reply. But the woman would be waiting until her china turned *two* centuries old if she expected Rachel to go along with this ridiculous idea.

Rachel needed to handle her refusal delicately, how-ever. Penelope Clayborn had been very patient with her niece's "brash Northern ways" so far—even though Rachel continued to speak familiarly with the servants, and, *heaven help us all,* wore only the "meagerest of pet-ticoats" beneath her dresses. But Rachel doubted the woman would be so patient if she rejected the notion of marrying Penelope's best friend's son without at least seeming to consider the idea.

Rachel smiled as sweetly as she could manage and cleared her throat. "I barely know anything about the man, Auntie." Well, that wasn't exactly the truth. Rachel knew Beau Bodain was weak-spirited, humorless, and conceited.

"But not knowing him gives you all the better reason to allow him to pay court to you, Rachel Ann. I'm sure you will find him an attentive, charming suitor."

Rachel looked down to keep from rolling her eyes in blatant disagreement. The two of them couldn't be talk-ing about the same man. "I'm not sure I'm ready to have suitors, Aunt Penelope. After all, I haven't even been accepted into polite society yet."

"Oh, nonsense, Rachel Ann," her aunt replied with a dismissive wave of her hand. "You are like the child Thomas and I never had, and this town has accepted you as such."

Accepted? That certainly wasn't the impression Rachel had gotten two days ago at church. There hadn't been a soul in attendance who'd wanted to sit beside her on a pew. They all called her the "Invading Yank," when they thought she wasn't listening, and she'd recently been the topic of more than a few unfounded rumors. She supposed it was all to be expected, though, considering she was fresh off the train from Ohio—and considering they were all a bunch of suspicious, narrow-minded Southerners.

"I'm not so convinced," Rachel replied. "Perhaps—"

Her aunt frowned. "If you are thinking of that unfortunate incident at church the other day, well that was simply a matter of politeness. The people of Glennville want to give you room to adjust."

"Aunt Penelope, the woman beside me refused to clasp my hand in prayer."

"But you must give them time, Rachel Ann," her aunt said with a frantic Southern twang. "I have no doubt that you will be completely accepted in time."

Certainly if I marry Beauregard Bodain, Rachel thought to herself. This was a point she was sure her aunt hadn't overlooked. What better way to be sure her niece was finally accepted than to marry her off to a bona fide Southern gentleman?

"Soon they will all come to realize that you, too, are a true Southerner," her aunt continued. "Good heavens, Rachel Ann, your mother was born and raised on this very plantation. That would bring dignity to the *lowest* bred Yankee."

Well, it was certainly good to know that she wasn't considered the *lowest*, Rachel thought dryly.

"Promise me you'll at least give the idea some thought," her aunt prodded.

"Of course I will, Auntie," Rachel replied sweetly. She'd dedicate exactly two seconds of thought to it that very night. And then she'd promptly forget the notion entirely.

"Good." Her aunt smiled. "Now what have you planned for the rest of the afternoon?"

"I thought a few quiet moments by the pond—"

"Heavens, Rachel Ann, that nasty pond again? I swear, the smell alone gives me the vapors. Why not spend the afternoon with your embroidery? Granny Mitzie tells me you're coming right along."

Granny Mitzie was Rachel's seventy-year-old great-grandmother on her mother's side. The woman had managed to outlive four husbands, eight children, and at last count, thirteen grandchildren. She was a walking curiosity and she could knit a collar around a running dog's neck in ten seconds flat.

"I prefer to take in a little air," Rachel replied, not willing to give up her plan of an afternoon in the sunshine.

"Oh, all right, then. But please try not to pinken your nose. I've arranged a small, last-minute dinner party this evening—"

Rachel shot the woman a startled glance.

"Don't give me that suspicious look, Rachel Ann."

"Tell me you didn't invite him, Aunt Penelope."

"I told you the best way to get to know Beauregard is to spend a little more time with him. Goodness," the woman said, laughing, "you'd think I'd invited a serpent to sit beside you at the table."

Rachel clenched her teeth in irritation. She would have *preferred* a serpent.

"Don't worry, I plan to see to it that you and Beauregard have plenty of time together."

That's what Rachel was afraid of. She wished she could shout right out that she would have nothing to do with Beauregard Bodain, but her situation offered her no such luxury. She would have to put up with every annoying thing her aunt chose to throw at her if she hoped to remain welcome in the woman's house.

What she needed to do was come up with some excuse that would allow her to gracefully bow out of this dinner party. Something polite. Something very, very Southern, like acquiring a headache that lasted three days, or having an attack of the vapors at dinner and fainting into a mashed-potato boat. She decided she'd spend her quiet time at the pond thinking about her options.

"If you'll excuse me, Aunt Penelope," she said, getting up from the settee, "I plan to take in some fresh air."

"Don't forget to take your parasol, Rachel Ann," her aunt called. "Heavens, the horrendous things that sun will do to your skin. Well, the possibilities would simply make you weak in the knees. Of course, a good cleansing with lemon juice—"

"Of course, Aunt Penelope," Rachel interrupted. Her smile was growing stiffer. "I would never leave my parasol behind."

Before her aunt could take another breath and continue with her classic dissertation about the sun and the high benefits of lemon juice, Rachel was heading across the foyer. She snatched a parasol out of the umbrella stand by the front door and escaped outside into the warmth of the sunny Georgia afternoon.

"Blasted woman," Rachel grumbled, popping open

the frilly white parasol. She'd spent the past two weeks in Penelope Clayborn's imperious presence—and she was damn near going mad!

She charged across the front porch, and almost ran smack dab into her uncle's wide back. He was standing on the top step, staring intently at the road stretching away from the house.

"Uncle Thomas?"

He startled slightly. "Good afternoon, Rachel Ann. You're certainly lookin' lovely today."

An amazing compliment considering he hadn't even looked at her yet. "What, exactly, are you doing?"

"I'm searchin' for dust clouds."

Rachel nodded. She'd always been aware that her aunt's husband was slightly eccentric, but this was downright odd. "And is this a particularly fine day for dust cloud watching?"

"It is if it indicates that that blasted captain has finally arrived."

Now Rachel understood. In order to run their cotton to England through Union lines, Glennville was in the process of purchasing their own fleet, their own block-ade runners. But their fearless captain was three days late, and the town was starting to squirm.

"Maybe he was captured at the blockade," she offered. Her uncle turned red in the face and scowled at her.

"Those dirty Yankees couldn't catch a cow standin' still, much less the slickest captain on the high seas!"

Rachel's nerves tightened, but she bit the inside of her lip and looked down to where her shoes were peek-ing out from beneath the hem of her white skirt. It was a humble stance, an uncharacteristic one for her, but it was the only way she could keep herself from shouting something insolent back at her uncle.

"The man will be here," he stated fiercely. "*He will be here!*"

Though she risked raising her uncle's wrath even more, Rachel couldn't walk away without inquiring about the fleet's status. "Have you and the others come up with the necessary funds?" she asked as gently and as sweetly as she could.

He turned to stare at the road. "We're workin' on it," he grumbled.

Which meant no. Managing a supportive smile, Rachel stepped down to the front drive. "I'm sure everything will work out, Uncle Thomas," she said.

At least for her everything would.

Scott sat in the tall grass out in the middle of nowhere with his head high and his legs stretched out in front of him. He had his eyes closed and one of his fingers resting on the end of his nose. The tests they were making him do fell just short of stupid. He kept telling them that, besides a momentary muscle weakness and slight dizziness, there were no side effects to traveling through time. But they always insisted on more tests to gauge his coordination and concentration levels.

What scientific genius was coming up with these things? They had him hopping on one foot while saying the Pledge of Allegiance, spinning in tight circles until he thought he'd puke, and now, sitting down with his eyes closed counting how many times he could touch his finger to his nose. He felt like a suspected drunk taking a roadside test.

He took out his data sheet, and beside the question of how many times he was able to connect his finger with his nose, he wrote: Plenty. He read onward to his next assignment and let out a groan. It read: *Listen to the audio tape on the Walkman provided and write down the words as you hear them.* "Christ," Scott grumbled. "Next they'll have me high-stepping to 'Singing in the Rain.'"

He pulled the Walkman out of his duffle bag and inserted the cassette. Then he broke into laughter. "Thanks, guys," he said. "Thanks a lot." It was Billy Ray Cyrus and his Achy Breaky Heart. It was a well-known fact among the participants of Stargazer that Scott Ramsey *hated* country music. It seemed Girney and his buddies had a sense of humor after all.

Scott could stand only two minutes of the tape before he turned it off and yanked the phones out of his ears. And when he reread the words he'd written down, he decided that he had good reason to hate country music.

His next assignment was a unique one, and he wondered if maybe it wasn't another joke. He was supposed to flip through the pages of a girlie magazine and measure his sexual response.

"You gotta be kidding," he said to himself. Did they literally mean "measure"? He glanced at his duffle bag, wondering if they'd provided him with a ruler. Or was he just supposed to guesstimate? he thought dryly.

"Christ," he muttered. He put the Walkman back into the duffle bag and fished around for the magazine. There was a particularly nice-looking, large-breasted blonde on the cover, and Scott arched his brows in approval. He supposed, joke or not, this could work itself up to be the best test yet.

He cracked open the magazine to the centerfold, and was proud to note a few moments later that he was already sprouting something measurable. . . .

"Hello."

Like a kid caught with his dad's "literature" in the bathroom, Scott quickly shut the magazine and jerked it behind his back. He'd been so enraptured with the amazing endowments of Miss May that he hadn't heard anyone approach. But he wasn't *supposed* to be approached, that's why he was always transported out into the middle of nowhere.

He slowly looked up, past yards and yards of white ruffled material, and found himself trapped in an inquisitive female stare; he sincerely hoped she hadn't gotten a look at what he'd been reading. Contact with locals hadn't exactly been a part of Scott's training, but he followed his instincts and smiled up at her.

"What are you doing here?" she asked.

He folded the magazine in half and tucked it into the back of his jeans. Then he stood, preparing to satisfy the nineteenth-century lady's curiosity and then send her on her way. But nothing could have prepared him for the impact of her beautiful face.

Her eyes were amazing, the palest most startling green he'd ever seen, and framed by a lush, dark fringe of lashes. She had ivory skin, a perfect nose, and delicate, full pink lips that should have drawn a crowd. The spark in her eyes told Scott that she was anything but your typical fragile beauty, however, and his smile broadened.

"Do you plan to answer me, or stand there grinning like a dumbstruck fool?"

Scott laughed at that comparison; dumbstruck was exactly how he felt.

"So you *do* have vocal capabilities," she remarked, a faint smile tugging at her own lips. "Next shall we try forming words?"

"I guess I'm just a little surprised to see you here."

"You expected me to be somewhere else?"

Maybe in heaven, he thought, letting his gaze roam appreciatively over her body from head to foot. "I'm surprised to see *anyone* here." He cocked his head at the puffy, frilly dress she was wearing; the skirt had to be the size and diameter of a small pup tent. "I must be lost," he added distractedly.

"And where were you going?"

Scott had to pause before answering, and that hesitation made her spectacular eyes narrow slightly. "Nowhere in particular," he finally replied. "I was just sitting here reading."

"I'd noticed." Her attention centered on his waist and she craned her neck to see what he'd hidden behind his back. "What was so important to read that it couldn't wait until you'd reached your destination of . . . nowhere in particular?"

Scott did a quick sidestep and reached behind him for the magazine. "You wouldn't be interested," he replied as he bent down and tucked it into his duffle bag. She frowned at the sound of him zipping the bag closed. "Trust me," he added, straightening and smiling at her again.

"Trust you?" she replied, looking skeptical. "When you won't even tell me where you're from?"

As if her appearance alone hadn't already wreaked enough havoc with his heart rate, her impish, crooked smile just about gave Scott a coronary. He felt like he was in grade school again, and Emily Anderson had just pinched his butt. "Where"—he was forced to clear his throat—"where exactly did *you* come from?" he finally managed to ask.

"*I* happen to live here," she replied. "And I am quite certain that you do not."

She lived here? That meant he was trespassing. Not a good development. "I see," he said, while trying to think up a good excuse for what the hell *he* was doing there.

"And now it's your turn." Her eyes sparkled like pale green crystal. "Where are *you* from?"

"I'm not exactly from around here."

"By the absence of your Southern accent, I'd already gathered that."

"And what can I gather from the absence of yours?"

"That I'm not a typical, naive Southern lady. Now, if you don't mind, I'd like some answers from you, sir, or I will be forced to report your presence here to my uncle. He doesn't appreciate trespassers."

Her uncle? Scott had a good five hours before the next portal opened, *if* it opened, and he wasn't too keen on spending that time running from some crazed plantation owner brandishing a pitchfork. "But I'm not bothering anybody."

"That remains to be seen," she replied, smiling crookedly again.

He smiled back. "Look, I didn't mean to trespass. I don't suppose you could you just let me rest here for a little while—?"

"Rest from what?"

She was quick, this one. And doggedly persistent. "From a very long trip."

"Which began when?"

"I'll be out of your hair in a couple of hours. I promise."

She frowned, looking confused, and reached up to toy with a piece of her hair.

"What I'm trying to say is—"

"What is your name?"

He hesitated again. "What does that matter?"

That had obviously been one evasive answer too many,

and, with a decided straightening of her narrow shoulders, she turned away from him. "I'd better get my uncle."

Impulsively, Scott lunged forward and took her by the arm. She let out a startled cry, but he drew her toward him. He had to convince her to let him go on about his business without telling anyone about his presence, otherwise he was bound to be asked more questions than he could successfully dodge.

What Scott didn't count on was the impact holding her close would have on his composure. She smelled like roses and rain, and the brush of her body against his made his skin tingle. "I can't let you do that," he said, his throat suddenly dry.

"Why not?"

She was staring up at him, her lush lips slightly parted, and Scott was suddenly seized by an almost overwhelming desire to kiss her. "I can't let you go."

Her eyes widened, and she glanced down at where his hand was wrapped around the entire circumference of her upper arm. "Then what, sir, do you intend to do with me?"

Now there was a loaded question. And Scott could think of about fifty different answers—all of them involving her and a lot less clothing. "If I let you go . . . will you promise to keep my presence here a secret?"

She swallowed, and he realized that she hadn't even tried to pull away from him. "Tell me who you are," she asked intently.

Hell, if that's all it would take to ensure her silence, Scott supposed he couldn't see any real harm in divulging his name. And maybe adding his rank to it would gain him just a little more of her trust. "Ramsey," he replied. "My name is Captain Scott Ramsey."

She went very still, her eyes searching his. "Captain Ramsey?" she repeated.

If Scott hadn't known any better he might have sworn she'd recognized his name. "That's right."

Suddenly her expression turned as hard and as cold as stone, and she went as rigid as a tree trunk. "So," she said through her teeth. "The pirate has finally arrived."

And without warning, she drew back her frilly umbrella and bashed him on the side of the head with it.

3

"If you do not let go of me, Captain, you will seriously regret it!"

The metal frame of Rachel's parasol had caught the man hard on the ear, and he'd let out quite a shout, but it hadn't been enough to make him release her. He'd simply torn the parasol out of her hand, and taken hold of *both* her arms.

"What are you gonna do now, lady? Pull a shotgun out of your knickers and blow me to hell!"

"Which is precisely where a wretched man like yourself belongs!" she shouted back. She tried to kick him in the shin, but he managed to avoid the sharp point of her shoe.

"Is this normal behavior for you?" he demanded, trying to control her violent squirming. "Or do you always turn on people like this!"

"Let go of me!" she cried.

But he did exactly the opposite: He wrapped his arms around her back and pulled her against his tall, hard body. This new position lessened the damage Rachel was capable of inflicting, but it only made her fight him more. Her breasts were smashed against his broad chest, and his hands were digging into her bottom through the many layers of her dress. The vile man's hips were digging into hers, and she couldn't so much as stomp on his toes in recompense.

Finally Rachel gave up on her efforts to free herself from his clutches. She was being mauled by a "dog of the sea," and if she ever hoped to survive the situation unscathed she would have to steady her nerves and think clearly.

How could she have been so stupid as to mistake him for a decent gentleman? But then he was as handsome as heaven—and certainly didn't *look* like a pirate! And that musky cologne he was wearing didn't make him *smell* like a pirate either. The man didn't even *talk* like a pirate, although some of the things he said did tend to be a little on the strange side. Who could possibly blame her for treating him as nicely as she had?

She could, that's who. Because she knew she'd been recklessly flirtatious with him for no other reason than that his very first smile had made her stomach do a flip-flop. His arms felt like steel bands around her, but he hadn't hurt her yet. And she had to believe that given the option he wouldn't. He was there to see her uncle, although he didn't seem aware that Thomas Clayborn *was* her uncle, or that he had indeed arrived at his intended destination. Perhaps informing him of these facts was all she needed to do to end this impromptu wrestling match between them.

"Do you ever intend to let me go?" she asked as calmly as she could.

He stared down into her face with dark eyes as fathomless as a midnight sky. No, he didn't look like a pirate at all, she realized as the warm summer breeze rustled through his dark-gold hair. He was far too handsome to be considered a sailing scourge. "Me letting you go all depends on you, lady," he said heatedly. "And on whether or not you've got any more of these interesting personality quirks itching to come lunging out at me."

"You should have told me from the very beginning that you were on your way to the plantation," she replied.

"The plantation?"

"That's right, Captain. You have arrived. *This* is Clayborn plantation."

His responding expression was nothing if not confused. "You sound as if you've been expecting me."

"Yes, well"—she gave him a tight smile—"secrets are hard to keep around here. Now, if you would be so kind as to let me go . . ." With a hard yank of her arms she finally managed to free herself and stumble a few steps back from his long reach. ". . . I'll take you to my uncle."

"I'd rather stay here."

She found herself glaring at him again. The last thing she wanted to do was introduce this man to her uncle, not when his very presence laid waste to weeks of careful planning. But she certainly couldn't leave him here and take the risk of her uncle finding out that he'd arrived and she'd neglected to bring him to the house. "You prefer a meadow to the comfort of a parlor chair?"

"Forgive me if I'm a little skeptical of your hospitality, lady, but one minute you're all smiles and charm, the next you're trying to bash my brains in with an umbrella, and now you're inviting me in for tea?"

Rachel was itching to tell him she wouldn't serve him tea if he were *shriveling* from thirst. But she'd learned to curb her tongue well during her time at the Clayborn's, and she knew that baiting the man now wouldn't do her any good at all—and might just land her on her uncle's bad side. "I'm afraid weak coffee is all we have," she replied with a tight smile.

"It doesn't matter. I'm not thirsty." And with that, he sat back down in the grass where she'd found him.

Rachel stared down at him in disbelief. Not ten seconds ago he'd been mauling her, demanding a promise in return for her freedom, and now he didn't seem to care whether she shouted his presence to the hilltops. "What happened to my all important silence?"

"You just told me I'm expected, although I don't have a clue why," he added with a mutter. "Tell your uncle I'll be there in about five hours."

"*Five hours*!" she exclaimed. "And what excuse do I give him for your delay?"

"Tell him I've got some business to attend to."

"Captain, I'm sure your business can wait," she replied. "And as for why I told you that you are expected, my uncle has been beside himself over this whole situation and I doubt he'd forgive me if I didn't bring you to the house immediately."

He looked up at her and shrugged. The sun shone down upon his tousled hair, creating streaks of pale gold, making him look almost angelic. Now *there* was a laughable image, Rachel thought. A pirate with a halo.

"My uncle was afraid that you and your crew might have been captured by Union merchantmen."

"My *crew*?"

"Yes, Captain. Your *ship* crew." A terrifying thought suddenly struck Rachel, and she glanced around the clearing. "You did come alone, didn't you?" The last thing she needed right now was to deal with ten more just like him.

He studied her carefully for a moment, and then said, "I came alone. Why is your uncle expecting me?"

"Because of your letter, of course."

"Of course."

"You told him that you planned to arrive in Savannah harbor this past Saturday with the ships, and that you would be arriving at his home to collect your ten thousand dollars."

Well that certainly seemed to get his attention, Rachel thought as his brows arched dramatically. "Ten thousand even?" he said.

It was obvious that he was expecting the full amount. However, as her uncle had admitted to her just that morning, the full ten thousand dollars had yet to be collected. And suddenly Rachel saw a golden opportunity to send this pagan pirate packing.

"Well . . ." she said, choosing her words carefully. "They don't exactly have the entire ten thousand. I believe it's more along the lines of eight."

She tried not to look too expectant as she stared down at him, tried not to seem as if she were hoping he'd jump to his feet and demand that she tell her uncle the bargain was off. But her announcement didn't seem to bother him in the slightest.

"In fact," she added, "I highly doubt that they'll be able to come up with any more than that at all."

There was still no reaction—the man was obviously slow-witted. "Considering the danger you and your crew will be in, Captain, no one would be at all surprised if you simply turned around and—"

"Rachel Ann! Rachel Ann Warren, where the devil have you gone off to?"

The sound of her uncle's booming voice sent Rachel's heart pounding. If he ever got even an inkling that she'd tried to discourage his pirate captain from staying, he'd have her packed and on the next train north by nightfall. "Of course my uncle would be horrified to know that I'd admitted his financial problems to you," she said quickly. "So, if you could refrain from telling him . . ." She bit her bottom lip. The captain was giving her the oddest look, and she realized that she was attempting to appeal to humanity where there was none. She was searching for charity from, of all things, a *pirate*.

Her uncle came toward them from the road. He was out of breath, and looked harried. "There you are, young lady. Your poor aunt has been callin' for you for over ten minutes. I suggest—" He paused, and frowned at the captain who was climbing to his feet. "Who is this young man?"

"Uncle Thomas," Rachel said, managing a tremulous smile. "I am pleased to introduce your captain. Mr. Scott Ramsey."

"*Ramsey*? I thought your name was *Remsby*."

"No, sir, it's Ramsey." The captain had an almost painful smile on his face as he held out his hand. "Captain Scott Ramsey."

Thomas Clayborn grunted, and then shook the man's hand. "I was beginnin' to give up on you, Captain."

"So I've heard." The captain glanced over at Rachel, and she cringed inwardly, praying he wouldn't mention a word of what she'd said about the fleet money.

"Well, come on up to the house and we'll talk," her uncle said. He looked around the clearing. "Where's your horse?"

The captain reached for his bag resting in the grass. "I don't have a horse."

Both Rachel and her uncle gave him a blank stare. He'd come all the way from Savannah harbor without a horse?

"Friendly folks, we Georgians," her uncle said, turning for the road. "Always willin' to give a stranger a ride. Come along, Rachel Ann. Mustn't lag behind."

Rachel snatched up her parasol and followed her uncle and his captain out of the meadow. She popped open the frilly parasol, not to block the sun but to use it to hide her interest in their conversation. If the captain decided to mention that she'd informed him of the fact that the money was not all gathered, then she was prepared to jump in and defend herself vigorously.

Her uncle was doing most of the talking, though, and the captain's answers were brief, almost vague. The man probably didn't give a fig about Glennville's cotton dilemma, or the South's "Cause." He was no doubt involved with the fleet for himself, and himself alone; a pirate to the core.

They entered the house and Rachel immediately dropped her parasol back into the umbrella stand. "Why don't you two have a seat in the parlor and I'll have Cassie bring you in some lemonade," she offered. That way she could listen in on their further conversation.

"Nonsense, Rachel Ann. The captain and I have business to discuss and shall do so in the study."

Rachel clenched her teeth as her uncle led the captain to the room at the right of the foyer. There were too many people in the house for her to risk listening at doors. She was just going to have to keep her fingers crossed and hope that she could count on the captain to be discreet about her behavior.

Realizing that she was once again relying on the pirate's charity, she groaned in frustration. Her only chance was to say some quick prayers and try to think up a proper explanation for why she'd tried to run off Glennville's last great hope.

*   *   *

Scott settled back in a high-backed leather chair and studied the room around him. Hardbound books lined the walls from floor to ceiling. Across from him was a gigantic window draped in gold velvet curtains. And in front of that was a large mahogany desk covered in nineteenth-century artifacts.

He studied Thomas Clayborn, who was leaning his mighty girth against the edge of the desk. Round. That was the only way to describe the man: round headed, round faced, and round bellied. His bristly white hair formed a horseshoe around his balding head, and his white, winged eyebrows almost completely covered his tiny blue eyes.

"We were expectin' you three days ago," Clayborn said. "We'd begun to suspect that the Yankees had intercepted you in Savannah harbor."

Scott didn't reply. He still hadn't quite figured out how to play this situation. He'd had little choice but to follow the man to his house, and now he wasn't at all sure what to expect from this unsmiling Southern gentleman who was mistaking him for a pirate.

"Did you bring the ships with you from St. George?" the man continued.

Scott still didn't respond, but he figured the man was referring to the ships the lovely Rachel had mentioned earlier.

"Captain, you did bring them didn't you?" Clayborn blustered. "You do realize that we are lost without them?"

In the face of the man's obvious desperation, Scott doubted this would be a good time to tell him that he wasn't a pirate captain and he didn't have any ships at all. But Clayborn was waiting for a reply, and Scott was going to have to say something eventually.

Then he remembered Rachel telling him that her uncle hadn't been able to come up with the full ten thousand dollars yet, and saw this as a possible way out. Of course she'd been downright desperate that he not let on to her uncle that she'd told him about the lack of money, so Scott knew he was going to have to tread carefully. "Have you got the money?" he asked softly.

The little round man began to squirm. "We, uh . . . we haven't yet gathered together the *full* amount agreed upon in your letter, Captain, but—"

"And when did you get my letter?" Scott interrupted. If he was going to pull this scheme off for the next few hours he was going to need to be as filled in as possible.

"Well, uh, let me see. . . ." Thomas Clayborn circled the desk, pulled open a drawer, and produced a folded piece of paper. "It's dated . . . it's dated May the fifth."

Scott reached for the letter, and the older man handed it across to him. It was written in an adolescent scrawl that was barely legible, but Scott did manage to discern a few words, such as Union blockade, three sleek frigates, and ten thousand dollars.

He skimmed down to the bottom of the letter, and could see why he'd been mistaken for this other captain. The signature, again hardly legible, read S. Remsby. At least that's what it looked like. It could have easily read S. Ramsey.

"Now there's no need to frown, Captain Ramsey. I promise you we will have the rest of your money in a matter of days. Those ships are very important to the planters of Glennville. Why, without them our cotton could spend the rest of the year in warehouses waitin' to be shipped to England."

"Cotton?" Scott replied distractedly, still trying to decipher the letter in his hand.

"Well, yes. Cotton. I explained it all very clearly to you in my initial letter. We want you to exchange our cotton for guns and ammunition."

And suddenly Scott began to realize what he'd stepped into. He gave Clayborn a steady look. "That's an interesting trade."

"I know, I know, we'll be givin' up a small fortune. But this damnable war has done more damage to the Southern economy than any of us could have ever dreamed. This plantation alone has had to sell half of its slave labor and put most of its house servants back to work in the fields. Our army needs more weapons, Captain, in order to end this unpleasantness once and for all. Only then can the South rise back to the greatness that it once was."

Wonderful, Scott thought dryly. *A man who sells human beings like Kool-Aid at a sidewalk stand.*

"In the name of the Confederacy, I am invitin' you to remain here as my honored guest while we gather the rest of your funds."

Scott fought the urge to laugh. He, a "pirate," was being invited to stay in the antebellum mansion of a Southern revolutionary to wait while ten thousand dollars was gathered in his name? He was certainly going to have some interesting stories to tell around the poker table that night. "How much more time do you need?" he asked.

"Two days, perhaps three. We're awaitin' word from a man in Atlanta who has shown an interest in our venture. Will you wait?"

Scott had a pretty good idea that a negative answer would get him tossed right out the front door—if not shot—while a polite and neighborly one would mean he'd have a nice comfortable place to stay for the next few hours while he waited for the time-portal. *And* he'd have an opportunity to spend more time with lovely, lively Rachel; he was dying to figure out what made that woman tick.

He smiled and stood from his chair. "Mr. Clayborn, I'd be happy to give you all the time you need."

The man sighed in relief. "Thank you, Captain. Your understandin' is greatly appreciated."

They shook hands, both of them smiling. But Scott doubted Thomas Clayborn would be quite so happy when in exactly four and a half hours his pirate captain disappeared without a trace.

4

"*I think the teal blue with the ivory* sash would be perfect."

Rachel nodded distractedly at her aunt, but her gaze was still glued to the study door across the foyer. She was doing her best to sit patiently on the settee in the parlor and wait for the outcome of her uncle's meeting with his captain, but the suspense was just about killing her. She'd thought up a few excuses for her behavior, but none of them were very founded, and she wasn't sure any would work on her stubborn-minded uncle.

"Of course that peach silk with the taffeta empire sleeves looks simply divine on you, Rachel Ann. . . . Rachel Ann?"

Hearing her name spoken in a louder tone of voice, Rachel pulled her attention to her aunt who was still sitting in the same Queen Anne chair she'd been sitting in earlier that afternoon. The woman had spent the entire day embroidering doilies for the lamp tables in the dining room, and the very idea made Rachel's eyes cross.

"Yes?" Rachel replied.

"I was wondering which gown you preferred to wear to dinner tonight."

Rachel gave her aunt a blank stare. Quite frankly, she couldn't have cared less. For her, the thrill of choosing a dress to wear was right up there with holding her pinky out when she drank tea, and keeping her skirt from bunching when she crossed her legs. "You choose," she said with an encouraging smile. "You're so much better at these things than I am."

"Well of course I am, my dear," her aunt replied, laughing softly. "I doubt you had much experience on that dreadful farm you grew up on."

Rachel's smile tightened. She hated this topic of discussion between her and her aunt, but the woman always found some way of bringing it up.

"Nonetheless," her aunt continued, "you are now a Southern girl, and will have to learn to make these important decisions."

Rachel looked away and rolled her eyes. Her aunt's version of an important decision didn't exactly correspond with hers.

"The Bodains and Trolleys will be arriving precisely at six, so be sure to have a little something to eat before then."

Ah, yes. We musn't forget to eat before *dinner, otherwise we might actually* consume *something in front of others. We wouldn't want to shock our auntie's friends, now would we?*

Actually, there was nothing Rachel would have liked more than to give her aunt's snobbish friends the vapors. She could only imagine what precious Mrs. Harmony Bodain would have done if *she'd* come across a pirate in a meadow as Rachel had done only that afternoon—

Rachel blinked, and then slowly began to smile. "Will Uncle Thomas's guest be joining us tonight?"

"His guest?"

"Captain Ramsey."

"That ship captain?" her aunt replied, looking shocked. "I can hardly imagine a man like that getting on at a dinner party full of decent, well-bred people, Rachel Ann. He'd probably insist on speaking about blockade running and booty gathering. No, I don't think so," she finished with a faint laugh.

But Rachel could imagine it very clearly. She felt that Captain Scott Ramsey was just what this little dinner party needed, and she intended to find a way to include the handsome pirate in the festivities—that is, if she was still welcome at the Clayborn's after his meeting with her uncle.

Her aunt went back to her embroidery, and Rachel stood up from the settee. The men had been shut up in the study for over fifteen minutes and it seemed like a blasted lifetime!

She strolled toward the parlor doorway, took a quick glance down the hallway, and then scooted across the foyer. Maybe if she stood close to the door she could overhear a little something.

Rachel hadn't gotten past the staircase before the study door opened and Captain Scott Ramsey walked out with her uncle right behind him. "Feel free to relax in the parlor," her uncle told him, "while I see about a room for you."

A room? Rachel thought. Dear Lord, the man was *staying*! Her uncle merely smiled at her as he turned and began climbing the staircase to the second floor. He would have wasted no time in confronting her if he knew of her behavior, so Rachel took it as a sign that the captain had said nothing untoward about her in the study. But she threw the pirate a suspicious glance, wondering why he'd refrained.

"Hi," he said, flashing her a smile. A smile she felt all the way down to her toes. "Exactly where is the parlor? We don't have them on pirate ships."

"Among other respectable things, I'm sure," she retorted. She was determined to resist the magnetic pull of his charm. "Follow me."

She led him into the room where her aunt was busy at work on her doilies and cleared her throat. This was one introduction she was going to enjoy immensely. "Penelope Clayborn," she said, "may I introduce Captain Scott Ramsey."

Her aunt looked up with a false smile on her lips. "I'm sorry, who, dear?"

"Ramsey, Auntie. Captain Scott Ramsey."

The woman's smile turned forced, and her throat spasmed as she swallowed down hard. "You're . . . you're that—"

"Pirate," Rachel replied. "Yes. Yes, he is."

The captain gave Penelope Clayborn a friendly smile. "It's a pleasure to meet you, ma'am."

Her aunt seemed to cringe away, even from the man's obvious charm, and, smiling to herself, Rachel backed up to the settee and sat down. "Do have a seat, Captain," Rachel invited.

She expected that he would take the wing chair beside her aunt, but instead he turned and joined her on the settee. In fact, he sat so close beside her that she was disconcerted to feel his thigh brush against hers.

She frowned down at the meager space between them, and then glanced up only to have her gaze slam directly into his. Her breath caught at the surprising warmth in his dark eyes, and then she quickly looked away, refocusing her attention back on her aunt who had turned such a pale shade of white that she was beginning to look blue. "You have a lovely home, Mrs. Clayborn," the captain said.

The man simply *oozed* manners, Rachel thought rancorously, but her aunt wasn't falling for his compliments. Penelope let out a gasp and began fanning herself with a half-embroidered doily, probably suspecting that the captain was sizing up her house for a robbery.

"There are valuables and priceless antiques in every room," Rachel stated with an overly proud smile.

"I've noticed," the captain replied, and Penelope Clayborn let out an audible groan.

"Perhaps you'd like a detailed tour?" Rachel asked.

"I'd love one."

"Good heavens!" Penelope Clayborn blurted, falling back into her chair.

"Are you all right, ma'am?"

"Everything is fine, Captain," Rachel replied over the gasping sounds of her aunt's fit of vapors.

"Maybe somebody should get her a glass of water."

"Aunt Penelope?" Rachel called. "Would you like the captain to get you a glass of water? Perhaps he could help loosen your stays a bit—"

"No!" the woman cried, holding out her hand. "I . . . I'll be fine. Just—just give me a few seconds to catch my breath."

"Are you sure?" Rachel asked.

"Quite—quite sure. Please . . . please stay where you are, Captain."

"She looks a little blue," the captain whispered.

"That's because she laces her stays too tight," Rachel whispered back. She gave her recovering aunt another bright smile. "Tell me, Captain, how was your visit with my uncle?" He took a moment to respond, and Rachel's attention was drawn back to his face, to his fathomless eyes.

"It was interesting."

"Really?" she replied. "And did he pay you the money for the ships?"

"He needs more time to collect the balance."

"Oh. But then that would mean you'd have to wait a few more days. Tell me, where will you be staying?"

He gave her a bewildered look, and she could only imagine what he was thinking. After all, she'd been standing right there when her uncle had said he would ready a room. "I'll be staying here," he replied.

Penelope Clayborn let out a sharp cry, and began fanning herself more vigorously.

"Maybe I should leave the room," the captain said, irritation lacing through his deep voice.

"Oh, no, please stay—Aunt Penelope, are you certain you'll be up to a dinner party tonight? I'm sure the captain wouldn't mind entertaining your guests in your absence."

That did it. With a loud moan and a flutter of her eyelashes, Penelope Clayborn collapsed into her chair in a dead faint.

Rachel couldn't help her broad grin. "Cassie!" she called. "Cassie, Mrs. Clayborn needs her smelling salts again!"

He'd never come across such a strange grouping of people before in his life.

Scott watched in stunned silence as a large black woman rushed into the parlor and knelt beside the ailing Penelope Clayborn. She waved a small vial beneath

Penelope's nose, and the woman slowly started to come around. He knew the old South had been populated by eccentric, socially obsessed people, but this was ridiculous. Penelope Clayborn didn't even know him, and she'd literally fainted at the idea of him *staying* in her house.

"Is she always this sensitive?" he asked Rachel, who was still seated beside him.

"Captain, you're in the South. It's practically written law that women be sensitive."

Rachel was still smiling, but Scott wasn't so sure he appreciated being used as a weapon against her fragile aunt. After all, he'd only been a pirate for the last half-hour, and hadn't had a chance to acquire the unfeeling black heart that reputedly came with the job.

"Are you feeling better yet, Auntie?"

The woman's eyes landed instantly on Scott, and he gave her a hesitant smile, afraid to make any sudden moves that might send her in a chair-to-floor nosedive. "Yes, I'm . . . feeling better," the woman replied weakly. "It's . . . it's grown rather warm in here. Cassie!" she snapped at the maid. "Open the windows for heaven's sake and let some air in here! Are you trying to suffocate us all, you old fool!"

Cassie went bustling to the other side of the room to do as she'd been commanded, and Scott suddenly wasn't feeling quite so bad about making Penelope Clayborn faint.

"Thank you, Cassie," Rachel said, once the slave had finished and was on her way out of the room. "I'll be up to dress in a few minutes."

"Yes'm, Miss Rachel," the woman replied.

Scott glanced at Rachel and saw that she was no longer smiling. She apparently didn't like the inconsiderate way the maid had just been treated any more than he did.

"Captain?" she asked, "do you have a change of clothes for the party tonight?"

"Rachel Ann—"

"Oh, I'm *sorry,* Auntie," she said coolly. "That was rather forward of me, wasn't it? I'm sure *Uncle Thomas* will see to the captain's clothing needs."

"What party?" Scott asked.

"The dinner party tonight. It's very small, actually, only a select number of people, but I'm sure you'll enjoy yourself, Captain."

Well *he* wasn't so sure, not if all of the women there were going to turn blue on him like Penelope Clayborn had done. In that case, he'd just as soon pass.

"Dinner will be served at six," Rachel told him.

And six was the exact time the portal was scheduled to reopen, so he supposed he was going to have to miss their little wing-ding.

"Aren't the other planters involved in the fleet purchase going to be there, Auntie?"

"Yes," the woman said in a wavering voice, although she did seem to be regaining some normal color. "Both Charles Bodain and Harold Trolley."

"You see, you can meet your other backers, Captain. Along with their lovely wives."

"Rachel Ann," Penelope Clayborn said quickly, "perhaps the captain isn't interested in attending one of our stuffy old parties. After all, the men will be speaking about planting and other such nonsense as that. The women will be discussing people he doesn't even know. And of course you and Beauregard—"

Rachel cleared her throat, loudly, and Scott gave her a curious sideways glance. "Beau and I shall be pursuing separate interests, I'm sure."

"My dear, acting coy with the young man will get you

absolutely nowhere. Beauregard told me himself only yesterday that he doesn't believe you like him very much at all. You must show him some sort of sign."

"Like a kick in the knee," Scott heard her mutter under her breath.

"What was that?" her aunt asked.

"I said . . . we'll have to see," Rachel replied, smiling tightly.

"That boy is the perfect match for you, my dear. And I intend to see to it that you have plenty of time this evening to discover that fact for yourself."

It was pretty plain to Scott that Rachel heartily disagreed. And she opened her mouth to respond, but her uncle came striding into the room at that moment. "Your accommodations are ready for you upstairs, Captain," he announced.

Just when things were starting to get interesting, Scott thought as he stood.

"Uncle Thomas, I've assured the captain that you will help him attain clothing suitable for the dinner party tonight."

"Party?" Thomas Clayborn said, frowning. "Oh, yes. Nearly forgot about that. Well, certainly. I'm sure we can find somethin' left by a previous guest that might fit you. Come along, Captain, and I'll show you to your room."

Scott chanced a polite nod at Penelope Clayborn, who was still looking at him as though she wanted to burrow through the back cushion on her chair and run for dear life, and then he turned to Rachel. She was looking expectantly up at him with those incredible pale eyes of hers.

"Until later tonight, Captain," she said, smiling brightly.

And, damn, if Scott didn't wish he could stay.

5

Rachel tried to take a deep breath but couldn't quite fill her lungs. "The blasted thing is too tight, Cassie," she complained, shoving at the corset beneath her dress. "Lord, I *hate* these things."

"Hold still an' let me pin up this last curl," the maid replied.

With a little advice from Cassie on the subject, Rachel had decided to wear the peach satin and taffeta dress. Not two hours ago she'd been trying to think up an excuse to bow out of this dinner party, and now she was having a hard time standing still long enough to get the final touches put to her hair.

"Girl, you are jigglin' like a bo-weevil in a corn patch. You best calm yourself, or you gonna end up with a pin stuck in the back a your head."

Rachel stared at her reflection in her full-length mirror and concentrated on not moving, but she absolutely had to be downstairs when her aunt was forced to introduce Captain Ramsey to her friends—and she was running out of time! "Hurry, Cassie, *hurry.*"

"Beauregard Bodain can wait five more seconds while I finish your hair."

Rachel scowled at the maid's reflection. "I don't give two hoots about Beauregard Bodain."

"That's not what your aunt says. She's been flutterin' round the house all day long, goin' on an' on 'bout how you's gonna finally unite the Clayborns and the Bodains."

"Well, I decline the honor, thank you very much."

With a chuckle, Cassie pressed a final pin into Rachel's hair and stepped back. "You don' *get* to decline, sugar. You get to *resign*. Resign yourself to the inev'table."

"Oh, isn't it enough that I've just about killed myself *re*learning how to walk, how to talk, how to balance a stupid teacup on my stupid knee?" Rachel replied. "Now I have to be led to the marriage altar like some sacrificial lamb?"

"Them other things was just the beginnin'. Now you got ta get yourself married up right, have a whole passel a babies, and then die young—while you're still pretty enough ta turn heads at your fun'ral."

Rachel let out a laugh. "That certainly does sum up the Southern female point of view."

"An speakin' a lookin' good, how 'bout that handsome man I saw you sittin' with this afternoon? Ummm-hm. He was a fine fella."

Rachel put on her best bland expression and fiddled with the edge of her peach satin sleeve. "Whoever do you mean?"

"You know who I mean. Lordy, that captain's got a smile that'll daze the fleas off a dog's *be*-hind."

"He's not from the South, you know," Rachel commented, casually adjusting the fit of her square-cut neckline. "He's only getting involved with the fleet for the money, not the 'Cause.'"

"*I* hear he's from some wild island out in the ocean."

"St. George." She arched a brow at the maid's reflection. "It's a *pirate's* haven."

"Oooh, don' you be usin' that word round your uncle or he'll whup your tiny behind."

Yes of course. In the North the common term was "pirate," but in the South the correct word to be used was "privateer." It was a much more delicate way of describing hired men who stole Northern ships and cargo, and then left entire crews for the sharks to feed on.

"You look perfect," Cassie told her, smiling brightly.

"Thank you." Rachel swayed her wide skirt a little.

"You're as purty as a silk-wrapped present."

Admiring her reflection, Rachel took a step backward to get a better look, but in doing so she gravely misjudged the weight of everything she was wearing. She stumbled, and then stepped on the side of her skirt. If it hadn't been for Cassie's quick response and strong arms, she would have gone toppling to the floor.

"Don' go killin' yourself before you even get down the stairs," the maid warned.

"A likely possibility," Rachel grumbled.

Cassie peered into her face. "You're lookin' a little pale," she said, and then gave each of Rachel's cheeks a good pinch.

"I'm pale because I can barely breathe in this contraption you strapped around my ribs."

"I told you, you have ta take slow, tiny breaths—"

"I don't *want* to learn to breathe differently! I don't *want* to learn to walk with a book on my head, or spend hours going blind over an embroidery needle!" Realizing what she was doing, Rachel let out a long sigh. "Oh, Cassie, I'm sorry. I don't know why I'm yelling at you."

"You feel better now?"

"A little," Rachel answered truthfully.

"Now take a moment ta catch your breath. You gotta keep from gettin' all worked up like this or you gonna faint for sure."

Rachel doubted that. She'd never fainted in her life—but then again she'd never had this much trouble breathing before either.

The clock on the mantel struck six o'clock, and Cassie went to open the door for her. "Practice takin' small, shallow breaths as you're walkin' down the stairs," the woman counseled.

"You mean as I'm *cartwheeling* down the stairs?"

The maid arched an impatient brow. "You gonna have a good night, or you gonna have a bad night?"

Remembering that although she was going to have to suffer through Beauregard Bodain's fumbled advances, she did have Captain Ramsey's attendance to look forward to, Rachel managed a smile. It was rather ironic, but since the captain's arrival that afternoon, her life had gotten eminently more interesting. "I suppose I should make the best of it," she replied.

"You're gonna be fine, Missy Rachel. Just fine."

Rachel kept telling herself that very thing on the walk from her room to the top of the stairs. A dinner party certainly wasn't going to kill her. Sure, she would have to suffer through a few exaggerated stories on the Southern war effort from the men's side of the table, look interested in a few dozen rumors about socialites gone awry from the women's side of the table, and carefully subvert any ideas that Beau Bodain might have taken into his overinflated head about a marriage between the two of them. But she did have the "scandalous" presence of Captain Ramsey to look forward to.

However, once the guests' initial reactions to the man had worn off, she was going to escape with a three-day headache the likes of which the South had never seen.

Unbeknownst to the dinner party gearing up downstairs, Scott was sitting in the middle of his bed, waiting for the time-portal. But his mind wasn't on returning home. No, he was thinking about Rachel, as he had done almost nonstop since meeting her that afternoon. She didn't quite fit in among these old-fashioned Southerners. In fact, he had a strong impression that she didn't even *like* her aunt.

What was she doing in Georgia when she was clearly from the North? Scott figured something must have happened to her family, forcing her to turn to the aid of relatives, but he couldn't believe that she'd willingly live south of the Mason-Dixon line. The woman was a puzzle he was dying to figure out, and it irritated him that he had to leave before he'd pieced everything about her together.

He leaned his head back against the headboard of his bed and tried to resign himself to his situation. This was not where he belonged, and he reminded himself of that while taking another long look around his room. It was twice the size of his bedroom back home. The bed looked like a priceless antique—an antique by 2001 standards, anyway—and he couldn't believe the size of the red marble fireplace. The damn thing was the width and breadth of a walk-in closet. He could have literally *stood* inside of it and built a fire. Scott was actually toying with the idea of getting up and trying the fireplace on for size when the seven-foot-high time-portal whirled open in front of the French doors a few feet away. He thought of Rachel one more time and felt regret tug at his insides. Then he took hold of his duffle bag and swung his legs over the side of the bed.

But then the damn portal started racing toward him like hell on wheels.

Out of pure instinct Scott pulled his legs up out of the way. The portal was swirling around like a cartoon imitation of its former passive self, and before Scott could even react, it had devoured the ladder-backed chair beside the nightstand beside the bed. Then, as quickly as it had arrived, the damn thing slammed shut again, leaving him sitting there with his legs in the air, looking totally astonished.

"Christ!" he cried, leaping off the bed. *Strengthened it,* they'd said. They'd turned it into a goddamn *Tazmanian Devil*!

He stared at the quiet room around him and threw his hands up in the air in disbelief. It would be another six hours before the door reset itself and returned to his location.

"Wonderful." He dropped back down onto the side of the bed. They should have at least warned him to be in the clear when the scheduled time came. Hell, they all knew that after one taste of anything solid the damn thing popped shut again in the blink of an eye—that had been one of the big screwups with the *first* mission. But it had certainly never come chasing after him quite like that before. He was obviously going to have be standing someplace completely vacant when the next portal opened.

For now, though, he thought irritably, all he could do was keep track of time and wait.

And then a smile crept over his face. This little catastrophe meant he had six more hours in which to avail himself of Rachel's intriguing presence. He lifted back his shirt cuff and checked his wristwatch. It was just after six. And he had a dinner party to attend.

Scott stood and looked down at the evening wear spread out on the foot of the bed and popped open the fly of his jeans. He was actually feeling excited about attending a soiree where he was probably going to be insulted and "cold-shouldered" all night long. He had to be out of his mind. But Rachel was definitely something worth getting excited over, and he pictured her mischievous smile as he sat down on the bed and pulled off his cowboy boots. He intended to lure her off into some quiet corner and spend a few nice long hours in her intriguing company before he left later that night.

He stood, slipped his jeans down his legs, picked up the heavy pair of black pants lying on the bed, and slipped them on over his boxers. He buttoned up the fly, then the two buttons on either side of the narrow waistband, and then shook out his legs.

The pants were a little baggier in the butt than he normally liked, but the real kicker was the length. The hem barely nudged his ankles.

"I don't think so," he muttered, and slipped the pants back off. His own jeans were going to have to do.

He looked down. Lying on the bed was the white shirt that he'd examined earlier. The thing didn't have *any* buttons. He'd been given a handful of shirt studs, but Scott figured his own shirt would suffice. So he pulled his jeans back on and tucked in his dark blue shirt.

He could see just by looking at it that the silk vest was too big, and it wasn't his style to wear one anyway, so he tossed that aside and picked up the black dinner jacket. He slipped his arms into it, adjusted his shirtsleeves, and wiggled his shoulders a little to get a feel for the fit. Then he stepped up to the full-length mirror to have a look at himself.

He didn't look half bad, he decided, tugging on the wide lapels, and then he sat in one of the chairs by the fireplace to pull his cowboy boots back on. What did it matter what he wore anyway? If Penelope Clayborn's guests were anything like the woman herself, he probably wouldn't cause much more of a stir if he showed up in a pair of tights and a tutu.

He ran his fingers through his hair, and then put his black bag next to the door for easy access in case he needed it quickly later on. Then he left his room for the party downstairs.

The long hallway was illuminated with stained glass kerosene lamps, and he counted four doors besides his own as he walked toward the staircase. Clayborn's house was nothing if not massive and opulent, and he couldn't believe the man was claiming war-torn poverty.

There was a woman standing at the top of the staircase, dressed in a peach-colored "Cinderella" dress, and as Scott drew closer he realized it was Rachel. She looked incredible, and distinctly as if she were struggling to breathe.

"Are you all right?" he asked, coming up beside her.

"I'm just trying . . . I'm just trying to catch my breath," she replied in a broken rasp. She was clinging to the banister. Her face was flushed, her lips were parted, and her full, firm breasts were heaving above the square, low-cut neckline of her dress.

Scott's physical reaction to her appearance was instantaneous, and he was glad he'd decided to button his long jacket. He reached out to steady her, but she moved back from his reach. "What the hell happened to you?" he demanded.

She glared at him. "My heel got caught in the carpet, Captain." She shoved furiously at her midsection. "I probably broke a rib."

"You fell?" he asked, concern tightening his stomach.

"*No,* I did not *fall.* I bent over to free my shoe, and . . . and this damn corset"—she shoved at her abdomen again —"stopped me cold. I swear I'm going to find the man who invented them and string him up by his—" She hesitated, and angled Scott a sideways look.

He arched a brow. "His thumbs?"

"Yes," she replied. "His thumbs."

"And what makes you think a *man* invented the corset?"

"Believe me, Captain, a woman would never do this to herself."

"And yet you wear it," he remarked.

Her responding stare was chilly. "Not without great duress, I assure you."

She cast a glance over what he was wearing, and then stuck her nose in the air and attempted to take the first step on the staircase. Her death-grip on the banister sort of ruined the contemptuous effect she was going for, though, and when she landed on the hem of her dress, she blew the moment completely.

"You're going to break your neck before you reach the bottom—"

"I'll be fine!"

Scott clenched his jaw and watched as she pulled in a disgruntled breath and tried the next step, only to have the same disastrous results as before. Finally, he stepped down beside her. "Give me your arm."

"I don't need your help—"

"*Give me your arm.*"

Though he could tell she resented his interference, she let go of the banister with her right hand and bent her elbow toward him. "This is really very unnecessary," she stated.

He took a light, but steady grip on the back of her elbow, and tried not to let the feel of her silky skin beneath his fingers distract him. "Hold up the front of the dress."

She hesitated, and Scott knew why. Holding up the front of her dress meant that she'd have to let go of the banister altogether, which meant she'd have to trust him to keep her balanced on the staircase. That was a lot for anybody to expect from a pirate.

"If you don't lift it you're going to end up stepping on it again—and then we'll both fall."

"Not if you let *me* fall," she retorted.

"Right," he replied. "And then I get blamed for pushing you and I hang at dawn. So don't think of this as me helping you down the stairs, think of this as me saving my own neck."

She looked up at him with those incredible eyes of hers and gave him an inquisitive stare that made him want to run his tongue along the fullness of her bottom lip. "Is that considered chivalry where you're from, Captain?"

He leaned closer, until he was torturing himself with her sweet breath on his face. "More like good common sense."

She considered him for a moment, stubbornly refusing to back down, and then pulled away to carefully raise her hand from the banister. "And what if I trip anyway and send us both tumbling?" she asked as she lifted the front of her skirt an inch or two.

"Then we can always use your dress as a parachute."

With his hand braced below her elbow, Scott began leading Rachel slowly down the stairs. She didn't say another word, and he tried to focus on the sound of her skirt rustling softly beside him, instead of the effect her nearness was having on his heart rate.

They made it to the bottom of the stairs in one piece, and Rachel said a soft thank you, moving out of his grasp as they touched down on the marble tiles of the foyer. She stayed close to his side, however, even when the two of them were spotted by the crowd in the parlor and two men, besides Thomas Clayborn, stepped out to greet them.

"Gentlemen," Clayborn said, "I believe you all know my niece Rachel Ann. And this is Captain Scott Ramsey. The man who is going to captain our ships through the Yankee blockade.

"Captain," Thomas Clayborn went on, "this is Harold Trolley. One of your backers."

Scott smiled and shook the hand of the man with the muttonchop sideburns, but the man never quite met his eyes.

"And this is Charles Bodain, another Glennville Fleet backer. Charles, this is Captain Ramsey."

Scott turned and shook the hand of the tall, graying man with spectacles perched on the end of his nose, and received a tremulous smirk in response to his friendly smile.

And then another younger man joined them. "This is my son, Captain," Charles Bodain said. "My son Beauregard."

"Beauregard," Scott said. He shook the thin blond man's hand, recognizing the name from Rachel's discussion with her aunt earlier that day. But Beauregard didn't seem to have any more backbone than the other men and barely met Scott's eyes.

And then Beauregard caught sight of Rachel standing a few feet away. As Beauregard moved forward toward

Rachel, Scott's first impulse was to step into his path, but he realized how ridiculous he was being when Rachel finally stepped forward and greeted the man.

"Good evening, Mr. Bodain."

"Miss Warren," Beauregard said in a breathy, nasal voice. "I do declare, the sight of you is like springtime in the winter."

Springtime in the winter? Christ, Scott thought, *who writes this guy's material?* And the guy wasn't just pale, he was pasty. His nose was too long for his narrow face. His lips were chapped, which meant he probably chewed on them when he got nervous. You'd think two wealthy people like Thomas and Penelope Clayborn could have found somebody better to date their niece.

Rachel was wearing a tight smile, which Scott thought looked more like a grimace. "How are you this evening, Mr. Bodain?" she asked.

"Enchanted," the man replied. "I am simply enchanted." He lifted Rachel's hand, turned it over ceremoniously, and placed a slobbery kiss on her palm.

Scott thought he might gag, but he smiled as Rachel pulled her hand back and furtively wiped it against the side of her skirt. It was pretty clear that she didn't like this man one damn bit.

"Penelope Clayborn, of course you're gonna introduce them," Scott heard Thomas Clayborn insist in a raspy whisper. He turned to see the pair standing close together a few feet away.

"But Thomas," the woman replied heatedly, "they don't want to be—"

She happened to look up at that moment and notice that Scott was watching them. Their conversation ceased, and she broke into a weak, false smile. "Captain," she said with a nervous shake in her voice.

Scott gave her a cool smile and looked away. He'd only been downstairs for two minutes, and already he was growing tired of everyone's chilly attitude toward him. Three women were standing in the parlor's double doorway, staring at him and beating fans at their necks as if they were trying to fly south for the winter, and he toyed with the idea of striding over and kissing them all full on the mouth. That would give them a little something to banter over tea.

"Captain," Thomas Clayborn said gruffly. "I'd like to introduce you to the women. Women," he added, "the captain. There. Now it's all settled. Let's head into the dinin' room, I'm half starved."

Everybody skirted past Scott in a quick beeline down the hallway, and he figured he could safely say that he'd never been treated so rudely in his life.

". . . Thank you, Beauregard, but I think I should allow the captain to escort me. He's standing all alone, and—"

"Nonsense, Rachel Ann. Your aunt informed me that it would be my honor to escort you to supper."

Scott angled Beauregard Bodain a sharp look as the man forcibly wrapped Rachel's arm through his and began leading her down the hall to the dining room. Again Scott had an urge to step into the matter, but just then a small, elderly woman dressed all in black stepped up to him.

"Hello!" she said loudly, and Scott was gifted with one of the few genuine smiles he'd received since his arrival.

"Hello," he replied, bemused.

"The name's Rothgate," the woman announced in a gravelly voice. "Mitzie Rothgate. And you may escort me in to supper."

The little woman took hold of his arm, before he even had a chance to reply, and began to drag him down the hallway. "Everybody calls me Granny Mitzie," she added. "And so will you or I'll box your ears."

Scott couldn't help but smile as he walked with the woman into the dining room. She reminded him a lot of his own grandmother, and for the first time since arriving that afternoon he actually felt comfortable.

He sat down at a long, oak table with fourteen chairs around it. Rachel was seated directly across from him and right next to Beauregard Bodain. "Granny Mitzie" was seated on Scott's left, and to the right was a pretty little blonde who couldn't seem to take her wide blue eyes off him.

Quiet conversation went on around the table as the first course was served by a stately looking black man who ladled them each a large bowl of tomato-based soup. Scott was starving, and tried to concentrate on eating despite the fact that all eyes were constantly leveling in his direction. He felt like an exotic animal on display.

"So you're the pirate," the old woman beside him suddenly stated loud and clear above the murmur of voices.

Scott heard a loud clatter of silverware against bowls as he paused over the last spoonful of his soup. He glanced down at the small woman hunched in the chair beside him, preparing to tell her that yes, that was exactly who he was, when Thomas Clayborn interrupted him.

"Granny Mitzie," Clayborn called from the head of the table. "Captain Ramsey is not a pirate. He is a *privateer*."

"Pirate, privateer," the old woman scoffed. "What's the difference?"

"The person who's addressing him," Rachel replied, and her uncle sent a dark scowl her way.

"Where's your ship?" Mitzie Rothgate demanded, staring up at Scott with sharp, tiny eyes.

"I left it in the ocean."

"And your scurvy crew?" she demanded.

"I left them on my scurvy ship." He smiled. "Somebody had to feed my scurvy dog."

The woman looked hard at him, a frown creasing her already wrinkled skin. And then she broke into deep-chested chuckles. "He's sharp as a whip!" she cried. "I like him! Pass the biscuits!"

A tentative silence fell over the table as everyone resumed their eating. Scott appreciated the fact that the old woman had taken a shine to him, but Rachel's opinion was the only one that really mattered. He just wished he knew what was going on behind those magnificent green eyes of hers.

"Captain?" Scott turned to the young woman seated on the other side of him. She was dressed in pale blue and her golden hair was styled in long sausage curls all over her head. She looked like a porcelain doll. "Have . . . have you ever been to China?" she asked, and two bright stains of red popped up on her cheeks.

"Melody Bodain," the blond woman down the table said in a warning voice. "Eat."

The young woman looked back down at her plate, but Scott decided to answer her anyway. "A few times," he replied. "What about you?"

"Been to India, have you?" Charles Bodain interrupted hastily, in an obvious attempt to shield his daughter from conversation with the dreaded pirate. As if Scott might dabble with the young lady's delectables right there on the sacred dinner table.

"No," Scott answered, "I've never been to India."

"How can you be a ship captain and have never gone

to India?" Beauregard Bodain replied with a haughty
laugh. "Am I right, Miss Warren?" he added, leaning so
far toward Rachel that she had to lean the other way to
avoid contact with his narrow little body.

"Simple," Scott wanted to say. "I'm not a ship captain, I'm an Air Force test pilot. And if you don't stop
brushing up against the woman sitting next to you I'm
gonna fly a big bad F-14 through the time-portal and
nuke your goddamn house." But Scott found he didn't
have to defend himself. *Rachel* came to his rescue.

"You know a lot about sailing, do you, Beauregard?"
she asked with a sweet little smile. "Please, do tell us all
about it."

Beauregard Bodain's expression went completely
blank and he began to stammer like a village idiot.

"My son is a planter," the blond woman who was
obviously Beauregard's mother replied regally from the
other end of the table. "He doesn't need to know about
the dangerous pursuits of sailing and the sea because he
shall always live off God's perfect land."

"Oh," Rachel replied. "I find it so boorish when a
man comments on the career of another man when he
hardly knows anything about it himself. Am I right,
Beauregard?" she asked, flashing that same sweet smile.

A tense moment of silence followed as Rachel went
back to her dinner and the rest of the table pretended as
if she hadn't just handed out the best damn put-down
any of them had heard in long time. Bodain's lips were
thinned and pale, and Scott thought he detected a slight
sheen of perspiration on the man's high forehead.

"Ummm . . . Beauregard?" Penelope Clayborn called
from the far end of the table. "It's such a lovely night.
Perhaps after dinner you and Rachel would enjoy a stroll
in the garden?"

"Well, that's a wonderful idea," Beauregard replied exuberantly. "What do you think, Miss Warren?"

From Scott's point of view *Miss Warren* suddenly looked as if she were about to be sick. "Actually," she replied, pressing her fingertips to her temples, "I'm afraid I'm coming down with a sizable headache."

"Then a little fresh air will certainly do you some good," her aunt replied.

Rachel's jaw tightened. Her aunt certainly seemed determined to fix her up with this cleft-chinned moron, and Scott was starting to feel a fair amount of irritation over the matter himself.

Rachel happened to glance in his direction at that moment and their gazes met. It was pretty plain that she was good and pissed about this stroll in the garden and if Scott planned to spend any time at all with her that evening, he was going to have to rescue her from the clutches of Beauregard Bodain.

6

Although she'd been faking it earlier, Rachel now had an honest-to-goodness headache.

At the behest of her aunt, she'd taken the required stroll through the garden in the moonlight with Beauregard, her Aunt Penelope and Harmony Bodain bringing up the rear as chaperones. Beau had told her how lovely she was, how witty she was, how lithesome and graceful she was, and had taken the opportunity to brush up against her as often as he could. Now they'd been left alone on the lamp-lit veranda to enjoy a quite moment of fresh air before Rachel retired for the evening.

She pulled her shawl more tightly around her shoulders, despite the warm night air, and leaned forward against the veranda railing. The moon was glowing like a giant white ball in the evening sky amid a field of twinkling stars, and she wished she could be enjoying the night alone—anywhere but where she was.

A pair of hands came down upon her shoulders and she closed her eyes in silent aggravation. Beau was being very persistent in his bid to court her, and she was running out of patience.

"It's a charming night," he said softly as he boldly pressed his body against her back. "A night for lovers in the moonlight."

Lovers? She sidestepped, and then turned to face him. A scathing reply to his brash statement was tickling the end of her tongue, and she wished she could give him a good piece of her mind once and for all. But the only recourse available to her was to politely excuse herself. "The nights here in Georgia are much warmer than I'm used to, Mr. Bodain," she said. "So I'm afraid that I will now—"

He smiled down at her. "The South is blessed to have you, Miss Warren. Anyone would be blessed to have you," he added with a twisted smile.

A shiver of distaste crept up Rachel's spine. "Mr. Bodain—"

"Beau."

"*Mr. Bodain*," she repeated. "I believe there is something you should know about me."

"Your beauty and your sweetness are all that matter." He reached for her hand.

Rachel took hold of the railing behind her to keep him from placing more slobbery kisses on her palm. "Mr. Bodain, I'm not interested in being courted by anyone at this time."

"Nonsense," he replied, moving closer. "Every girl needs a beau."

"Not this girl," she replied quickly.

"But your aunt told me—"

"Never mind what my aunt said. I am telling you that I'm not prepared to court at this time."

He seemed taken aback, and Rachel prayed that she

had finally gotten through to him. "Well, what do you mean, not at this time? When *will* you be interested?"

In you? she thought. *I wouldn't hold your breath, my friend.* "I'm not sure," she hedged.

"My mother isn't going to like this," he said, frowning. "She was hoping we'd be married by the end of summer."

The very idea almost made Rachel burst into laughter. "Then you will simply have to explain to her that I—"

"Allow me to tell her that you've agreed to consent to my suit at a later date."

Rachel's first impulse was to refuse, but she hesitated. Her aunt certainly wasn't going to take this news any better than Beau's mother. Her best bet for any peace at all during the rest of her stay at the plantation was if she gave them something to hope for.

"All right," she finally agreed. "But you have to give me at least another month before you bother—before you *approach* me about this again."

"It's a deal," he stated. Then he smiled. "And now," he added, leaning closer, "let's seal our bargain with a kiss."

Before Rachel could cringe away from him, Beau pulled her up against his chest and smashed his moist lips against her mouth. Horror made her heart pound, which made her breath quicken, which made her corset squeeze tighter, which made her head go slightly dizzy—

And then a throat cleared a few feet away from them.

Beau instantly straightened, and Rachel stole the opportunity to scoot out from between him and the railing he'd trapped her against.

"Sorry to interrupt, but your father's looking for you, Beauregard."

It was Captain Ramsey's voice that was coming from the shadows, and Rachel's heart started to pound all over again. "Then . . . then certainly, Mr. Bodain," she said breathlessly, "you must hurry and see what he wants."

Beau scowled at the captain's silhouette, and Rachel caught a flash of the pirate's broad smile in the moonlight. It had been fairly apparent during dinner that the two men disliked each other, and Rachel had to admit that she admired the captain's good sense.

Beau offered her his arm. "Come along, Miss Warren."

The very thought of touching him again made Rachel cling to the veranda railing. "You go on ahead, Mr. Bodain. I'm going to enjoy the night air a little longer."

"But, Miss Warren," Beau said softly, "you can't stay out here alone with this man."

It *was* a little on the daring side, but Rachel felt that if the captain planned to attack her he would have done so before now. "I intend to remain outside *alone*, Mr. Bodain. If the captain intends to do the same, then there is hardly anything I can say about the matter."

Beau pursed his lips in obvious agitation. "Captain Ramsey? Are you coming in then?"

"It's a nice night," the captain replied. "I think I'll stay."

"A true gentleman does not stand alone in the dark with an unattached lady," Beau stated.

"Then I guess that counts us both out, doesn't it, Beauregard?"

"Are you insulting my honor, sir?"

"Now why would I do something as dangerous as that?" That reply seemed to pacify Beau, even though Rachel could tell the captain was being sarcastic.

"Very well," Beau replied stiffly. "But I suggest you keep your distance from the young lady, or I shall be forced to take offense."

With that rather ridiculous threat hanging in the air, Beauregard Bodain turned and strode across the veranda and into the parlor through the open French doors.

"I'll be sure to keep that in mind," the captain muttered dryly. He walked toward Rachel out of the shadows and into the soft moonlight. "Is this the kind of behavior we can expect from all your boyfriends?"

Rachel let out a weary sigh and leaned back against the railing. "Beauregard Bodain and I are *not* friends, Captain."

"I think somebody needs to tell *him* that."

"Was his father really looking for him, or was your intention merely to send him packing?" she asked, suspicious of his timely appearance.

"Would you care either way?"

He was standing directly in front of her now, staring at her with dark shadowed eyes, and it surprised Rachel how easily he could undermine her composure. She tried to remind herself of who he was—of what he was—but the effort was lost in the moonlight. "What . . . what could be your reason for luring him into the house?"

"It didn't look as if you were enjoying his fumbled advances."

Her face heated at the realization that he'd seen them kissing, and her humiliation ignited a spark of anger within her. "Considering your background, I'm surprised you weren't interested in prolonging the show," she retorted.

"I guess I'm a pirate with a heart of gold."

"More like a *thirst* for gold."

"Save the ice-princess attitude, Rachel, you don't have to be embarrassed by what I saw. It's not your fault Beauregard has seventeen hands."

She narrowed her eyes on his face, hating that he'd read her emotions so easily. "My *attitude* has nothing to do with embarrassment, Captain, and everything to do with my intense dislike of *you*."

"You don't even know me," he responded.

"I know all I need to know."

She attempted to brush past him for the door, but he caught her by the arm and pulled her back in front of him. "You mean everything you've concluded on your own?"

"I think your profession and reputation speak for themselves," she replied, "now let go of my arm."

Surprisingly, he did as she asked, but he planted his tall, broad body directly in her path to the door. "Somehow I thought you'd be more tolerant than this."

Rachel gritted her teeth. "Tolerant of a bloodthirsty pirate?" she retorted vehemently. "A man who would sell his mother's soul for money?"

"So *that's* why everybody was so rude to me tonight at dinner. I've supposedly sold my own mother's soul."

She scowled at his sarcasm. "And what did you expect? That they'd welcome you into their fold with open arms?"

"Oh, I doubt those people would recognize goodwill if it climbed up their legs and bit them on their Southern asses. So we've established the various reasons behind my shunning. But why were they so rude to *you*?"

"I beg your pardon?"

"It's just that I noticed none of the ladies came forward to say hello to you when we walked down into the foyer. And they didn't exactly go out of their way to engage you in their discussions during dinner."

Rachel didn't like the direction their conversation was turning. So she too was being shunned by the imperious citizens of Glennville? What business was that of his?

"Hm," he grunted. "By the expression on your face you must have done something pretty terrible yourself."

"I haven't done anything wrong!" she snapped. "These blasted people don't even know . . . me." By the time she'd finished her sentence, she'd realized what the captain had done. He'd turned her own intolerance around on her. "That is certainly not the same thing!"

"Oh, I think it is," he replied, chuckling. "How does it feel to be unjustifiably judged, Rachel? Frustrating, isn't it?"

"You're a devil," she ground out. "And a pirate. And I don't need proof to know that you raid and kill—"

He was shaking his head. "I don't do that." She gave him a skeptical look and he smiled. "I delegate all that messy stuff to my scurvy crew."

"Are you trying to be funny?"

"Rachel," he said seriously, "I am not the man you think I am."

"I don't believe you. I don't believe a word you're saying!"

"Have I ever lied to you?"

"Well, that's a ridiculous question considering we met only four short hours ago and I hardly know—" She cut herself off short, but he'd heard her loud and clear.

"I believe that's another point for my team," he said, smirking.

She clenched her jaw. "You are the most annoying—"

"And you are incredibly beautiful."

His unexpected compliment startled her, as did the sincerity with which he'd said it, and she blinked in surprise. She'd certainly heard the words before, from Beau, in fact, just a little while ago, but she'd never had them said to her with such raw candor.

"That's an odd thing to say at a time like this," she replied.

"I didn't say it to make you uncomfortable."

"Then what, exactly, did you mean to do?"

"You don't have to worry," he replied, smiling, "I don't intend to pin you against the railing and force myself on you."

"The man barely even kissed me!" she retorted.

"Then he's more of an idiot than I thought."

Her heart lurched unexpectedly and she actually wished that he would stop complimenting her so brazenly. He was gazing intently down into her eyes, his warm breath a soft caress against her face, and it was then that she realized how very close he was standing to her. She told herself she should move back, put some distance between their bodies, but she felt rooted to the spot, snared in the web of his seductive charm.

His lips, full and strong, drew her attention, and her breath quickened. She was suddenly, unequivocally longing for his kiss, knowing instinctively that it would be like none she had ever experienced.

"The eyes are the window to the soul, Rachel," he said softly.

She wanted to reply, but it was taking every ounce of her strength and concentration not to throw her arms around his neck and pull his mouth to hers.

"They'll always give you away."

She wasn't quite sure what he meant, but his words frightened her just the same; the last thing in the world she could afford to be was transparent.

He cupped her cheeks with his hands. His palms were warm against her skin. Her eyes continued to linger over his parted lips, and she wondered what would happen if she gave in to the urge to taste them just this once.

"But can we stop at just one kiss?" he whispered.

The man had practically read her mind. Her breathing went crazy. Her heart hammered in her chest, and she raised her hand to her constricted ribs to try to catch her breath, but realized she couldn't.

Noticing her difficulty, the captain peered into her face. "Are you all right?"

Rachel couldn't answer.

"Rachel?" he persisted. "You sound like you're hyperventilating."

"My . . . my corset . . ." she managed to gasp.

She grew dizzy and the captain took her by the shoulders. Concern was digging a deep groove between his eyebrows, but Rachel could only watch helplessly as his handsome face blurred from her vision. And then she slipped into the comforting arms of unconsciousness.

Scott had had some interesting things happen to him with women before, but he could safely say that none had ever fainted on him.

He'd merely wanted a little kiss, nothing elaborate, nothing too aggressive, and he could have sworn he'd seen the same desire sparkling in Rachel's eyes. But then she'd clutched at her ribs and collapsed in his arms.

She was as white as a sheet, and he carefully lowered her to the veranda deck to try patting her cheeks to bring her around. Her breathing was quick and shallow, and he set his hand on her abdomen to better gauge her respiration.

Instead of giving into soft, female flesh, Scott's hand landed on something stiff and immovable beneath her dress. The corset. She'd said she couldn't breathe, and he now remembered that she'd had the same problem on the stairs earlier that evening.

His first impulse was to get the thing off her, and so he immediately started searching the front of her dress for buttons. There weren't any buttons, though, so he rolled her to her side and searched the back of her dress. He couldn't find any buttons there either.

"Was she born in the goddamn thing?" he muttered.

The neckline of the dress was too small to pull down, the waist was too tight to pull up, and so Scott hovered over her in frustration.

And that's when his attempt at first aid turned into something a whole lot more interesting.

Her long, smooth arms came up and twined around his neck, pulling him closer. Her full lips parted, and he found himself being drawn down to her mouth. Resisting was certainly the last thing on his mind, so he pulled her up tightly against him for a soul-stirring kiss.

Her soft lips moved silkenly beneath his as he tasted her. She was warm, and sweet, sighing into his mouth, and Scott soon forgot where he was.

Leave it to Beauregard Bodain to remind him.

"Now see here, Ramsey!" Beauregard shouted in a high-pitched squeak from above them. "This kind of action will not be tolerated!"

The lips beneath Scott's suddenly went rigid, and Scott regretfully pulled away. Rachel's expression was shadowed by the darkness, but he could imagine the embarrassment this was going to cause her. And when the lady got embarrassed, the lady got mad, and her anger was no doubt going to be aimed directly at him.

He took a moment to steady his nerves before sitting back on his heels. Beauregard looked as though he were expecting an explanation, but Scott had no intention of explaining himself to the man. He rose to his feet and offered his hand to Rachel.

She refused to take it, instead climbing to her feet by use of the veranda railing. The moonlight reflected in her eyes as she turned toward him, and had Scott been made of ice he would have been liquefied on the spot. He itched to point out to her that it had been *she* who'd kissed *him*, not the other way around, but he doubted it would make a bit of difference to her at the moment.

The entire dinner party had come out onto the veranda, and Bodain was now pointing an accusing finger at Scott. "This man has overstepped the lines of decency—"

For Rachel's sake, it now seemed prudent for Scott to offer some sort of explanation. "Cool your jets, Bodain—"

"It's all perfectly innocent," Rachel announced, her voice wavering slightly. "I fainted and—"

"No doubt because of his scurrilous advances! I demand an immediate apology from this man!"

Before Scott could ask why Bodain should get the apology and not Rachel, Thomas Clayborn stepped forward with a dark frown on his round face.

"I fainted, Uncle Thomas," Rachel insisted. "Mr. Bodain is making far too much of this."

"*Do* something, Thomas," Penelope Clayborn insisted, her fan moving rapidly at her neck. "Remove this . . . this reprobate from our home!"

Scott became the object of Thomas Clayborn's considering stare, and he knew the man was weighing his options. To get rid of his pirate captain would mean the end of his precious fleet. But to not get rid of the pirate captain might mean the end of his niece's reputation.

Thomas Clayborn cleared his throat. "I'm sure it's just

as Rachel has said," he announced. "She fainted, and the captain was . . . was merely helpin' her to her feet."

And the fleet is the apparent winner, Scott thought with a strange mixture of relief and disgust.

But Beauregard wasn't ready to let the matter rest. "What I saw was not—"

"Are you callin' my niece a liar, Bodain?" Clayborn interrupted, drilling the younger man with a sharp glare.

Bodain pursed his lips. "Fine," he said. "But I must now *insist* that Rachel come into the house with the rest of us."

"And I have every intention of doing so," Rachel replied. She marched across the veranda without giving Scott so much as a glance, and he had to fight the urge to charge forward like some Neanderthal and stop her. Once she cooled off, she'd realize that she'd been just as much a part of that kiss as he had. The problem was, he might not be around long enough to witness her change of heart.

"Got a game of poker startin' up in a few minutes," Thomas Clayborn said.

Scott kept his eyes on Rachel as she slipped into the house with the rest of the dinner party. "What's your point, Clayborn?" he replied, his mood less than companionable.

"I was wonderin' if you'd care to participate, Captain. The stakes are a meager few dollars, and possibly a bit of thrashed pride."

Scott gave the man his full attention. "Will Beauregard Bodain be joining us?"

"Yes, sir, I believe he will be."

"Then you can count me in." He smiled coldly. "I'm in the mood for a good thrashing."

7

If she could round up all the men in the world and stuff them into a small bag, she'd toss them all into Savannah harbor and whistle "Yankee Doodle" as she sauntered merrily away.

In fact, that was what Rachel was imagining as she dragged a brush through her hair. She didn't know who she was more aggravated with, Captain Ramsey or herself. She'd fainted—for the very first time in her life, and had she been awakened by the pungent odor of smelling salts? No. Had she opened her eyes to the concerned faces of her family and friends? No. She'd been unceremoniously attacked by that immoral pirate! And then she'd actually had to defend his actions in order to save herself!

The fact that she'd enjoyed his kiss was beside the point. He'd taken advantage of her at a very delicate moment—just like the scoundrel she'd assumed all along that he was.

A sharp knock came at her door and she started badly enough to drop her brush. She couldn't imagine who would be knocking on her door at this late hour, but the first possible person who popped into her mind was the captain. Would the man actually have the audacity to sneak upstairs to her room after what he'd already put her through? Well, this time she would scream! She would scream his blasted *ears* off!

She stood from her dressing table, slipped her arms into her robe, and marched toward the door. If it *was* him, she planned to give him a solid piece of her mind before she slammed the door in his face. "Who is it?" she demanded, holding tightly to the knob.

"It is I, your aunt Penelope. Please allow me entrance."

Rachel rolled her eyes. She didn't like the sound of her aunt's voice one bit. That tight, haughty tone usually meant a lecture, and Rachel certainly wasn't in the mood for one at the moment. But, knowing she couldn't send her aunt scurrying as she'd hoped to do to the captain, she opened the door.

Her aunt Penelope breezed into the room still wearing her lime green evening gown. "Certainly, Rachel Ann, you *know* what this means."

Rachel let out a frustrated sigh and shut her door. "No, Aunt Penelope, I have no idea." *But I'm sure you're going to tell me,* she added to herself.

"You and Beauregard can simply not afford to wait."

"Wait for what?"

"I talked with Harmony before she and Melody left and she completely agrees with me."

Rachel grew nervous at that point. Anytime Penelope Clayborn and Harmony Bodain put their heads together it made her very, *very* nervous. "What are you talking about, Aunt Penelope?"

"Why, you and Beauregard of course," the woman replied, stooping to pick Rachel's brush up off the floor.

"You've been compromised. You can't possibly think that this kind of scandal won't get out."

"There was no scandal," Rachel insisted. "I fainted. The captain was simply helping me to my feet. Aunt Penelope, Beauregard mistook what he saw."

"Goodness, my dear," her aunt said, laughing faintly, "your cheeks were as hot as twin suns when I arrived on the veranda. I don't believe *any* of us mistook what we saw."

"But I—"

"No buts. Your reputation is at stake. As is mine and your uncle's. We simply cannot let this pass without taking some sort of action. I have already instructed Harmony that Beauregard may call upon you in the morning."

"*Not on your life!*" Rachel shouted without thinking.

Her aunt froze, her expression turning instantly glacial. "Do not *shriek* at me, young lady."

"I'm sorry," Rachel replied more calmly, remembering her role as the docile niece. "But there simply has to be another answer."

"This is the only acceptable one."

Rachel leaned back against the door, her feelings of frustration beginning to overcome her. *Oh I don't know,* she thought bitterly. *Shooting myself is still an option.*

"And if you're going to be upset with someone, I suggest you aim your slings and arrows directly at Captain Ramsey. It is solely because of him that your reputation needs reconciling."

And her aunt and haughty Harmony were taking grand advantage of that fact, weren't they?

"You will be up and dressed to go riding by a quarter of ten, Rachel Ann. Don't make me come looking for you." Rachel moved so her aunt could open the door.

"Have a good night's rest," Penelope said. "I'm sure things will look much brighter in the morning."

Gritting her teeth, Rachel closed the door solidly behind her aunt. "Things couldn't look brighter with a sky full of *fire*," she muttered angrily. She strode over to her dressing table, picked up her hairbrush, and threw it across the room. "Where does that woman get the nerve to tell me who will call on me and when! So I kissed a pirate!" she continued furiously. "It was one little kiss! One simple little kiss! And now I'm supposed to pay for it by playing lovebirds with that pale-faced popinjay! Talk about adding insult to injury!"

She flopped down, face-first, on her bed and tried to calm herself, but she'd never been so enraged in her life. She *hated* the South! Hated their ridiculous customs that overlooked the most basic rules of fairness! Good Lord, how she longed to return home to Ohio where reason and understanding prevailed!

She'd stayed far too long in Glennville, that was her problem. Which led her right back to that despicable captain, Scott Ramsey. She had to find the safe containing the fleet money before her uncle raised the balance he owed. Otherwise Thomas Clayborn was going to give the money to that blasted pirate—and Rachel would no doubt have one hell of a time stealing it from *him*.

She'd already searched every room in the house, though—every room except her uncle's study. And tonight she intended to do just that. With any luck at all she'd find what she'd been searching two long weeks for, and then rid herself of the South and all its glory once and for all!

*   *   *

He couldn't wait to get away from this pompous bunch of windbags. In fact, if the time-portal had shown up right then and there, Scott would have thrown caution to the wind and stepped right on through to home.

He was sitting at a circular card table watching his four opponents carefully. Thomas had loaned him five dollars with which to play, and that bankroll had quickly increased itself to forty confederate dollars—to the great disdain of everyone else at the table. Scott hadn't quite figured out if they were pissed about losing to a pirate, or just plain pissed about losing.

Harold Trolley threw his cards down onto the table. "I fold," he grumbled.

Scott turned his eyes to Charles Bodain. The man considered him for a moment, then looked at Scott's cards as if he might be able to see through the paper, and then tossed down his hand too. "I'm out."

With a grunt and a flick of his wrist, Thomas Clayborn did the same, and now all eyes turned to Beauregard Bodain, who was systematically devouring his own bottom lip. He looked at Scott, then glanced at his cards, then he looked at Scott, and glanced at the pile of money in the center of the table.

Come on, Bodain, Scott thought to himself. *Be a smart boy and toss in your cards.* Beauregard had challenged him in almost every hand that night. And Beauregard had lost every single time.

"This time I think he's bluffing," Beauregard finally blurted. He tossed a large confederate dollar bill into the pot and laid his card hand on the table. He had a pair of kings.

Scott sighed, looked Beauregard in the eye, and turned over his own hand. "Straight to the queen."

"Damn!" Bodain shouted, slamming his palm down on the table. "Damn, damn, damn!"

Scott leaned forward and scooped up his winnings. "I rarely ever bluff, Bodain."

"But I'm sure you cheat like the very dickens!" Everyone else around the table shifted uncomfortably, and cast disbelieving glances at the man. "Oh, I don't care if he's a bloodthirsty villain!" Beauregard shouted at them. "I say he's cheating!"

"I don't have to cheat to beat you, Bodain," Scott replied.

The man's small blue eyes narrowed, and Scott gave him a cool smile, hoping he might finally get an opportunity to pop the bastard. The man had been asking for it all night long. Thomas Clayborn cleared his throat. "I believe it's your deal, Trolley."

Scott kept his steady stare on Beauregard while piling his fifty or so one-dollar bills into a neat stack. Then he pushed back his chair, scraping it loudly against the wood plank floor. "I'm out," he announced.

"Oh, that's just fine!" Beauregard shouted. "Quit before we even have a chance to earn back your ill-gotten gains—"

Scott lunged across the table toward the man. "If you've got a problem with me, Bodain, then maybe we should take it outside?"

Beau Bodain pressed back in his chair, his lips quivering in quiet fury as Scott waited eagerly for a sign, *any* sign. But Beauregard disappointed him by backing down. "A . . . a gentleman does not resort to fisticuffs."

His bespectacled father patted him on the back. "Why don't you go on out front and get yourself some fresh air, son?"

"Yes," Beauregard replied, scooting back his chair. "I . . . I believe I'll do that."

Scott turned away from the table and headed for the

sideboard to pour himself a drink. He checked his watch for the tenth time as he sat down on a tall stool. It was eleven-thirty. Thirty more minutes before the portal arrived and he still hadn't worked up the courage to go upstairs and say good-bye to Rachel.

She couldn't still be mad at him. Hell, she'd had over two hours to cool off. But the idea of his final memory of her being a heated argument had kept him from heading upstairs to find out for himself.

Of course he could always return home without seeing her again. But the thought of that made him feel sick to his stomach. No, he'd say his good-byes, and then he'd go home and dream about her for the rest of his damn life.

Time passed so slowly that Rachel could have sworn the seconds were ticking off like minutes. When eleven-thirty finally arrived, she eased into her white cambric robe and quietly left her room. She tiptoed her way carefully down the long, dark hallway, and once she'd reached the top of the staircase, paused to listen for any sounds coming from below. Nothing but quiet filled the house.

She hurried down the stairs to the foyer and pressed herself up against the study door. Her heart was racing so fast she could almost hear her own blood swooshing in her ears. There was a low murmur of male voices coming from the game room at the back of the house, and she hoped desperately that they would all stay put until she'd found what she was searching for.

She reached behind her and turned the knob of the study door. Then she quietly slipped inside the darkened room.

The curtains on the large picture window had been

left open, providing ample moonlight for her to find the match safe on the desk and light a candle. She began her search with the desk drawers. There were three along each side, and she spent the next ten minutes sifting through papers, account books, and ledgers, looking for a cash box. But she found nothing of the kind.

Next she moved to the pictures hanging on the wall, looking behind each one for a hidden safe. But she found nothing there either.

"Damn," she muttered, blowing a piece of dark hair back out of her eyes. The money *had* to be there. She'd looked everywhere else!

She stood in the center of the room and studied the bookcases; there could be a hidden safe behind any one of them. It would take her quite some time to check every shelf, but, considering she wasn't going home until she'd found the money, she really had no other choice.

She decided to start with the shelf along the far wall since it had the most moonlight shining on it. She crossed the floor toward it, and stumbled over the edge of the Oriental carpet. She stopped and stared down at her feet, realizing floorboards could be pried up and a safe hidden beneath.

Taking the candle from the desk, she crouched beside the rug, pulled back an edge, and began running her fingers over the wood planks. One of the boards creaked, moving beneath her fingers, and she broke out in a triumphant smile. She set the candle aside and carefully pried up a board. Three others rose with it on a well-oiled hinge and Rachel pulled the candle closer to stare down at the safe hidden in the floor.

"Very clever, Uncle Thomas," she whispered.

She stared at the combination dial, and tried to imagine

what sequence of numbers her uncle would use to lock up his valuables. She tried her aunt's birthday, and when that failed she thought a moment more. "Oh! It would be his *own* birthday, of course!"

A few moments later the lock clicked, and Rachel's heart thumped. She turned the handle, slowly lifted the heavy metal door, and spied stacks of confederate money stashed inside. Victory at last. Nothing could stop her now.

"What are you doing?"

Forget the question, the voice itself startled Rachel so badly she knocked over the candle sitting beside her. She fumbled in the dark and managed to close the safe, spin the dial, and lower the hinged floorboards. Then she turned to see a shadowy figure leaning back against the study door.

One of the men had come into the room while she'd had her nose stuck down into her uncle's safe. He moved into the moonlight, and she caught her breath. He was the very last man she wanted to see.

Scott excused himself from the game room at a quarter to twelve. He climbed the stairs to his bedroom, retrieved his duffle bag, and headed for Rachel's room at the end of the opposite hall.

His hand was actually shaking as he knocked softly on her door. He wasn't sure what explanation he was going to give her for leaving so unexpectedly, he just knew he wasn't going anywhere until he'd seen her one last time.

She didn't answer his knock. He took a chance and turned the knob, easing open the door to peer inside. The lamp was still lit by the bedside, but the bed and the room were both empty.

Frowning, he pulled the door closed. Where the hell would she have gone in the middle of the night?

He headed for the staircase, knowing he was running out of time. The house was darker than he remembered when he'd been hurrying up the stairs, and it was in that moment that he saw the glow of light coming from beneath the door to the study.

He crossed the foyer toward the room and carefully eased open the door. He wasn't sure what he expected to find, but what he saw crouched in the middle of the study floor surprised him. It was Rachel. And she was definitely up to something.

"What are you doing?" he asked softly while shutting the door behind him.

His question startled her so badly that she knocked over the candle beside her, pitching the room into blackness. He heard a frantic fumbling, and assumed she was trying to relight the candle. So he moved closer, into the moonlight, to reassure her.

She gasped at the sight of him. "What are you doing in here?" she demanded in a whisper.

"What are *you* doing in here?"

"I . . . I lost an earring," she replied, straightening the rug back out over the floor.

"You lost an earring *under* the rug?"

"It's a very *small* earring," she replied tightly. She stood up in front of him and he saw that she was dressed in a filmy white nightgown and robe. "It could have rolled anywhere," she added.

Scott detected a faint tremor in her voice, and began to get the distinct impression that she was lying to him. But the last thing in the world he wanted to do at the moment was put her on guard, so he smiled and moved closer, until the sweet, gentle fragrance of her perfume tickled his nose. "Maybe you lost it on the veranda when you threw yourself into my arms."

Even in the meager moonlight he could see the glow of her pale green eyes as she narrowed them on him. "I fainted, Captain. Let's be sure we keep that perfectly clear. I fainted, and you took advantage of me."

So she still hadn't gotten over it. "Rachel, we both know that's not true."

"Like hell, Captain," she hissed. "One moment I was floating in oblivion, and then next thing I knew you were kissing me."

Scott studied her for a moment and realized she believed what she was saying. She apparently had no recollection of wrapping her arms around his neck and pulling him to her. "You remember the *kiss* don't you?" Christ, *he'd* never forget it.

"Of course I do," she said, looking away. "How could I forget the most *humiliating* moment of my life."

That was a direct hit to his pride, and Scott was starting to get a little irritated himself. "If it was so terrible, then what the hell was that vise-grip you had on my neck?"

"I fainted," she snapped. "I was *completely* out of my wits."

"And acting on instinct, I take it?" he taunted.

She glared hard at him. "What kind of a man takes advantage of a woman like that, Captain? A scurrilous, amoral pirate, perhaps?"

Direct hit number two. "I wouldn't know, sweetheart. Attacking coldhearted virgins isn't my style."

He'd had enough of this heartfelt good-bye, and turned to leave, but, in a surprising move, she took him by the lapels of his borrowed jacket and pulled him back toward her. "Don't you *dare* tell my uncle about my being in here tonight!"

"And why would he care?"

"He wouldn't," she said quickly. "That's why I'm insisting you not bother him about it."

Right, Scott thought. The woman was definitely up to something, and he figured it was about time he got some straight answers from her. He pressed closer to her, making her grip on his jacket unnecessary, but she still held on to him. "It sounds to me like you're *afraid* of him finding out you were here."

Her eyes darted away from his as she tried to come up with a suitable reply. "If you must know," she finally said, "my uncle considers his study his sanctuary. I don't think he'd appreciate me snooping around in here for an earring."

"Or just plain snooping around?"

She went still against him. "Are you *accusing* me of something, Captain?"

Scott wasn't quite prepared to do that, so he bent forward, forcing her to lean back over the desk as he stared down into her eyes. "Why are you so desperate for my cooperation?"

Her eyes widened. "I . . . I am no such thing."

"Then why are you still holding on to my jacket?"

She looked down at her hands as if just now remembering they were still gripping his lapels. Her fists slackened, but to keep her from completely letting go of him he pressed himself more tightly against her. He could feel the rapid rise and fall of her soft breasts beneath her thin nightgown, and instantly his body remembered what it felt like to hold her in his arms, to have her clinging to his neck and wanting his kiss. He wrapped his arms around her.

"What are you doing?" she whispered, her voice shaking a bit.

"I'm kissing you, Rachel."

He captured her lips in a breathless moment that shut out the rest of the world. She sank into his embrace, sighing into his mouth, and slowly but surely her hands crept up his arms, over his shoulders, and twined around his neck. She arched against him, sending sparks shooting through his stomach as he fitted her body to his. He nibbled at her lips, coaxed them apart, and then allowed himself a long leisurely taste of her mouth. This attraction he felt for her was insane but impossible to resist. And with a groan of resignation, Scott finally stopped trying.

He sank his hands into the thin material of her robe, molding his fingers to the curves of her firm backside, and lifted her up against him to feel the lush, soft pressure of her breasts pressed to his chest. He sat her down on the edge of the desk, preparing to make this a farewell neither one of them would ever forget. He was tugging her robe and nightgown from her shoulder when they both heard the voice of her uncle in the hallway outside.

". . . to find it, Harold. Perhaps you left it in the study."

Rachel's gasp moved Scott into action as heavy footsteps approached the study. He took her around the waist and hauled her to the far corner beside the door. It wasn't until the knob began to creak that he spotted his duffle bag by the chair. He lunged forward, snatched it up, and then pressed Rachel back against the wall behind him.

The door swung open and Scott held his breath as it nearly hit him in the face. The squatty form of Thomas Clayborn sauntered into the room, moving toward the desk. "Where the hell is the candlestick?" Clayborn muttered, and Scott felt Rachel stiffen behind him.

"Damn servants. They've scrambled everything around on my desk again."

"Did you find it, Thomas?" Harold Trolley called from the hallway.

"'Fraid not," Clayborn called back. He muttered something else unintelligible, and left the room, shutting the door tightly behind him. "I'll have to look for it tomorrow in the good light."

Scott let go of the breath he'd been holding, and felt Rachel relax behind him. He wasn't sure what Clayborn would have done had he found his fleet captain ensconced in the dark with his niece, but Scott felt pretty sure it wouldn't have gone well for either of them. She began shoving at his back, and he was about to step away from her when he heard the unmistakable whir of the time-portal opening. Even in the dark he could see it, spinning to life across the room by the desk. "Damn," he muttered. He'd completely lost track of time.

"What's that noise?" Rachel demanded in a whisper, her fingers sinking into the back of his jacket.

"Just the wind," Scott replied as the time-portal began racing toward him with all the velocity and determination of a Kansas tornado. How in the hell was he going to get through it without Rachel seeing? Even now she was shoving at his back, demanding that he move away so she could get a look at what was making all the noise.

And then the entire dilemma was solved. The damn thing sucked up the globe and stand sitting beside the desk and closed without him once again.

"Move away from me, you oversized clod!" Rachel demanded and gave him one good final shove. With a disgruntled sigh, Scott finally moved, and she stepped out from behind him. "What was that noise?" she demanded again.

"I told you, it was the wind."

"There's no wind outside, Captain. And the window is closed."

"Then you've got a better explanation?" he replied.

Rachel stood quietly for a moment, probably trying to determine whether or not he was lying to her, and then stepped toward the desk. "My uncle didn't see us, did he?"

"I'm sure he would have said something if he had."

"I certainly hope . . ." She paused, frowning down at the spot where the globe and stand had been. "I certainly hope you're right, or I'll probably be *engaged* by this time tomorrow."

Scott was also staring at the spot where the globe and stand had been, where the portal had closed. He was nagged with the notion that something hadn't been quite right. There had been something different about the damn thing, something besides its new velocity.

"You can go up to your room now," Rachel said to him. "I'll be fine here by myself."

He gave her a surprised look. "You're staying?"

"I still need to find my earring, Captain."

"Right. Your earring. Well, hell. I've got time. What say I help you look?"

"After what just happened between us, Captain, I'm sure you'll understand if I prefer to do it by myself." The moonlight was reflecting off the back of her head, hiding her eyes from him, but Scott could still make out the determined jut of her chin.

"And what just happened?" he prodded.

"You kissed me."

"*I* kissed you."

"We kissed . . . we kissed each other. Reason enough for us both to stay clear of one another from now on."

"That's funny," he said, walking toward her. "I see it as the exact opposite."

She backed away from him so fast she slammed into the desk. "On second thought, I suppose I can look for my earring tomorrow when the light is better."

And before Scott could reply she'd dashed across the room and slipped out the door. He smiled after her, but then turned back to the place where the globe had been standing. He crouched down beside the desk to get a better look, measuring with his eyes. The entire globe and stand had been about four feet high, yet it had fit snugly within the time portal.

"Christ," Scott whispered.

Now he knew what had been so different. His ride home was shrinking.

8

The time-portal opened at precisely six-seventeen the next morning, and Scott's worst suspicions were confirmed. The damn thing was malfunctioning again.

He wadded up a message he'd written for Colonel Tayback, explaining the problem and asking to have someone check on his grandmother, and tossed it through the tiny portal that was now down to the size of a small cupboard.

He had no idea how long it would take them to fix it. All he could do was sit tight. And wait.

Rachel opened her eyes just as the bright glow of the morning sun touched the beveled glass of her windowpane. She immediately threw back the covers and swung her legs over the side of the bed. She had an appointment to keep, and needed to sneak out of the house before her aunt and uncle awakened.

She got out of bed and hurried toward the washbasin where she rinsed her face and freshened her mouth. Then she dressed in a plain gray skirt and a white ruffled shirt, purposefully avoiding corsets and petticoats; she'd need none of that this morning.

She pulled on her stockings and shoes, and then ran a quick brush through her hair. By the time the clock on her mantel chimed six-thirty she had quietly slipped out of her bedroom.

The west hallway was as empty as it had been the night before, but still she treaded carefully down the carpet runner toward the staircase. Her aunt and uncle rarely rose before nine, early by Southern standards, but the house servants were usually up by dawn.

Dishes clanked in the kitchen at the back of the house, and Rachel was careful to avoid the squeaky stair as she descended toward the foyer. She cast a longing glance at the study doors, but knew it was too dangerous to attempt to steal the money in the light of day. She had no choice but to wait until that night, thanks to Captain Scott Ramsey and his blasted kisses.

She glanced both ways at the bottom of the stairs and then darted for the front door.

"Where you off ta in such a hurry?"

Rachel froze with her hand on the doorknob. Then she turned, slowly, to face the formidable Cassie. The maid was scowling at her, and Rachel supposed it had been too much to hope that she could sneak out of the house every three days to meet her contacts and never be caught.

"And what the *dickens* is you wearin', girl?"

Thinking quickly, Rachel broke into her sweetest smile. "Something comfortable, Cassie. I thought I'd take a little stroll before breakfast."

"Before breakfast?" the woman stated incredulously. "You up before the *good Lord* has even opened *His* eyes!"

"Shhhh!" Rachel whispered, hurrying toward the maid. "I've spent my entire life on a farm where it's considered commendable to rise before the rooster, Cassie. Old habits are very hard to break."

The maid's ebony brows knitted. "Your aunt is gonna ride you up one side and down t'other if she sees you leavin' this house dressed half naked like you are."

"I am not—" Rachel began defensively, and then she paused and took a deep breath. *Calm,* she reminded herself. *Remain calm.* "You know as well as I do that I am not half naked. Besides, how could Aunt Penelope possibly find out what I wore beneath my dress this morning . . . unless, of course, you tell her."

"*I* ain't lyin' to that woman!" Cassie cried.

"I am not asking you to lie. I am simply suggesting that you don't *offer* her the truth."

The maid's scowl turned deliberating. "You ain't plannin' on leavin' the property, is ya? If anybody catches sight a you—"

"I am going for a quiet walk by the pond," Rachel lied.

"Your aunt hates you playin' out in the sun at that pond—"

Rachel strode to the umbrella stand and lifted out a blue frilly parasol. "Consider me well armed."

The maid frowned at her for a moment, and then shook her head. "I guess I certainly can't stop ya," she grumbled, turning back toward the kitchen. "Doubt a whole herd a elephants could stop that girl."

Before Cassie could change her mind, Rachel pulled the front door open and hurried out into the warm morning sunshine. She didn't even bother to open the parasol as she scampered down the road toward the pond. She was running behind schedule, and the consequences could be dire if she were late.

She arrived at the tangle of blackberry bushes that circled the pond, and then turned down the path that headed along the west end of her uncle's property. That's when she heard the distinct sound of male singing.

"I'd like to take a rocket to the moon. . . ."

Rachel's first impulse was to run as far and as fast as she could. But as the man continued singing the odd song, she began to recognize the deep resonance of his voice. "I'd like to split bananas with an old baboon. . . ."

Burning with curiosity, Rachel moved a few feet down the hedge and peeked through a thinning in the tangle of vines and leaves. What she saw made her eyes go wide and pulled a soft gasp from her throat.

"I'd like to see December. . . ."

It was the captain. The man was bathing, *naked,* in the pond!

". . . in the month of June. . . ."

She quickly considered her options. She could follow her first impulse and run like the wind. Or she could stand here like a shameless hussy and watch the man romp in the water. Without further consideration, she pressed her face back to the opening in the hedge.

"But most of all I'd like to be with you, you, you. . . ."

She stared, unblinking, at Scott Ramsey's broad, muscular back. His powerful shoulders were rippling in the sunshine as he scrubbed each of his arms with a wet cloth. She could see the curve of his spine all the way to the top of his buttocks, and her cheeks went hot at the sight.

"Yeah, most of all I'd like to be with you."

He turned in her direction and began scrubbing his chest. He had a rich golden tan that covered his body, and a heavy, warm sensation grew in the pit of Rachel's belly.

"I'd like to swing like Tarzan through the trees. . . ."

He was completely unaware that she was standing there, staring at him like a smitten schoolgirl. She wondered what he'd do if he looked up and discovered her watching him, and the idea made her heart pound even more.

"And take a walk through gallon crates of fresh-shucked peas. . . ."

And then he started walking toward her.

"Good Lord," she whispered to herself, as he began to rise up from the water like a golden Adonis. He had muscles where she never knew muscles existed. And she was tingling in places she never knew she had.

She stared in astonishment as he rose above the water level, revealing his rigid abdomen. Her eyes grew wider and wider. He was gradually exposing himself to her, teasing her senses, leaving her mouth dry with anticipation. And then a twig snapped beneath her foot. The captain froze, and Rachel held her breath in horror. "Who's there?" he called out.

Rachel hiked up her skirt and took off in a dead run. The captain called out, but she ignored him, knowing he hadn't seen her and hoping to keep it that way. But as she fled down the path, she knew she'd never in her entire life forget the sight of his wet powerful body rising up from that water.

She ran until she thought her lungs would burst, and then finally stopped to catch her breath. That's when she realized she'd left her parasol behind by the black-berry bushes. Closing her eyes, she prayed silently that the captain wouldn't find it. As it was, she wasn't sure she'd ever be able to look him in the eye again.

She continued in the direction of the large fallen tree that had been her assigned meeting place for the past two weeks. When she arrived, she saw that her two contacts were already there waiting, dressed in civilian attire.

"Where the hell have you been, Rachel Ann?" Jeremy demanded the moment he saw her.

"I got here as fast as I could, Jeremy." She dropped down beside Zach on the horizontal tree, and hoped that the color in her cheeks wouldn't raise their curiosities any higher.

"You were supposed to be here over twenty minutes ago," Jeremy continued angrily.

"I was detained at the house by an overprotective maid."

"You know we worry about you, Rachel Ann," Zach said softly.

"Our agreement was that you report, *punctually,* every three days, or we bundle you up and take you back home."

Rachel gritted her teeth. How *could* she forget that agreement? They lorded it over her head every chance they got. "I'm sorry," she replied impatiently. "What more do you want me to say?"

Jeremy's green eyes glittered. "That you'll follow orders like a good little spy, and be punctual to your debriefings."

"Neither one of us likes lying in our bedrolls at night thinking our little sister is in danger," Zach added. "Tell us you've finally found the money so we can return you to the proper side of the Mason-Dixon."

"I have," she said.

"You have?" Jeremy repeated in shock.

"Of course. I said I would, didn't I? Even though the two of you have doubted me from the very beginning, Uncle Thomas hasn't suspected me for one moment." She arched her brows. "I doubt either of you would have been able to claim such a thing at this point."

Her brothers were continuing to exchange surprised looks, and Rachel was beginning to feel very smug. She'd always been so jealous of their commissions to help defend the Union, and when news of her uncle's plan to buy weapons for the South had first reached her family she'd immediately offered up a plan to take care of the matter. Her brothers had thought her idea ludicrous. "A *woman* spy?" they'd both said incredulously.

But General James Garfield hadn't agreed with their narrow-minded opinions. He'd thought her plan to pretend defection to the South was an excellent idea, and agreed with her that no one would suspect her as a Union spy.

Of course, Rachel's parents didn't like the idea one bit, but anyone who knew Rachel Ann Warren knew that trying to talk her out of something once she'd set her mind to it was like trying to convince the wind to stop blowing.

Only a few days later Rachel had received her orders from the general himself, and her brothers had no choice but to escort her to Georgia.

"Stop gloating and tell us what you did with the money," Jeremy said.

"Nothing."

"Nothing?" Zach repeated.

"I left it in the safe in Uncle Thomas's study."

"What!" Jeremy exclaimed. "You've been searching for that cash for over two weeks, all of us putting our lives in danger, Rachel Ann, and you left it in the safe!"

"What if he moves it?" Zach asked.

That had been Rachel's single greatest fear since leaving it in the study the night before—blast that damn Captain Ramsey!—but she certainly wasn't going to let her brothers know that. "Don't be ridiculous," she replied. "Why on earth would he move it now? He's waiting for some banker in Atlanta to send him the rest of the money he needs, and that will take at *least* another couple of days." She glared at Jeremy. "So stop shouting at me!"

"Why didn't you just take it and leave last night?" he demanded.

"Because I was interrupted."

"By Uncle Thomas?" Zach suddenly looked concerned.

"No . . . By Captain Ramsey."

Jeremy scowled. "Captain Ramsey?"

"The pirate captain Uncle Thomas has hired to sail the fleet. He arrived yesterday afternoon."

"Damn it," Jeremy swore. "And he agreed to wait for the rest of the money, I suppose?"

"He's staying at the house."

"A pirate in Aunt Penelope's house?" Zach broke into a grin. "Ah, to be a fly on the wall."

"It has been rather interesting," Rachel replied.

Jeremy was scowling again. "You've got to get that money before Uncle Thomas gives it to him, Rachel."

"I know that," she snapped. "I'm not a complete *idiot*, Jeremy. I'm going back into the study tonight."

"What did the captain do when he found you rifling Uncle Thomas's safe?"

Rachel hesitated. Leave it to Zach, the scamp, to ask such a loaded question. "It was dark. He didn't realize what I was doing."

"Well, what did you tell him?" Jeremy asked.

"I told him I was looking for a lost earring."

He arched a dark brow at her. "And he believed you?"

"He offered to help me look. I declined and left the room." *End of story, end of topic,* she added to herself. "I'll have the money and be leaving by first light tomorrow."

"You're going to break darling Beauregard's heart," Zach said with a twisted smile.

Rachel rolled her eyes. "We're going riding together this morning. Dare I hope I'll break a leg walking back to the house and be unable to attend?"

"You're letting him court you?" Jeremy replied, surprised.

"Our dictatorial aunt has given me little choice. After the incident on the veranda last night—"

"What incident?" Zach asked.

Realizing what she'd let slip, Rachel raised her chin. "I fainted on the veranda."

"You *what*?" Zach replied incredulously. "You've never fainted in your life."

"And I've never worn a corset before either," she quickly pointed out. "I'd like to see either of you strap one of those horrendous things on and survive an evening of snobbery and gossip."

"It sounds to me as if you don't like our lovely aunt and her charming friends," Zach said.

"Let's just say I'll be happy to return home."

"Maybe the life of a spy's too much for her," Jeremy remarked.

"Without me, Jeremy David Warren, you'd still be kissing the toes of our uncle's boots trying to find enough favor with him to earn yourself the run of his house."

Jeremy studied her for a moment, and then nodded. "Okay, little sister. I admit that you've done a good job. But I'll sleep much better once we get you back to Ohio where you belong."

So will I, Rachel thought to herself. She'd had enough of the spy business to last her a lifetime.

Zach rose up from the fallen tree and went to stand beside Jeremy. "Good work," he said to her. "We're proud of you."

"But the most dangerous part is still to come," Jeremy reminded them. "Remember. Take this path to the hunter's cottage. It's about five miles down the way and hidden in the trees, so watch for it. People are going to begin looking for you once it's discovered that you're gone, so Zach and I will have to wait until it's dark before meeting you there. Just stay quiet and you'll be fine."

Rachel nodded, excitement beginning to pulse through her veins. Tonight she would steal the money and end her stay at the Clayborns. No more lying and pretending, no more smiling sweetly until her cheeks hurt. One more day and she would be going home.

Scott strode toward the house, his damp hair dripping down the sides of his neck. He was swinging the parasol he'd found behind the blackberry bushes at the pond. Thomas Clayborn was sitting on the veranda in a rattan chair, sipping a steaming drink. "Have you seen Rachel?" Scott asked.

The man looked up at him. "Good mornin', Captain. No, no, I haven't seen Rachel Ann yet today. Have a seat and I'll have Moses fetch you some coffee."

Clayborn reached for the silver bell sitting on the small table beside him, but Scott held up his hand. "I'm fine." If he needed coffee, he'd damn well go into the kitchen and get it himself. He laid the parasol along the top of the railing and reached up to brush away a droplet of water running down his neck.

"Afraid of gettin' too much sun?" Clayborn inquired, nodding toward the parasol.

"I found it by the pond. I assume it's your niece's."

Clayborn nodded. "Probably."

Scott turned and looked out over the garden. He couldn't believe it. Rachel had actually spied on him while he was taking a bath! The woman was just one surprise after another.

Footsteps on the veranda stairs caught his attention. He turned, and there she was, a tangle of wildflowers clutched in her hand. God help him, she looked incredible. Her eyes were glowing, her dark hair was hanging loose, and there was a fresh rosy hue to her cheeks. Any man would have to be insane not to find her completely breathtaking.

"Out gatherin' foliage again, I see," her uncle remarked.

"I like vases of flowers in my room," she replied. She gave Scott a hesitant glance. "Captain, I'm—" Her attention caught on the frilly blue parasol lying on the railing. Scott watched her complexion go from rosy, to pale, to downright flammable.

"You're what?" he asked casually. Ashamed? Embarrassed? Dare he hope *intrigued*?

She looked away, her mouth working in a drawn-out stammer. "I . . . I'm—I'm surprised to see you up and about so early."

He was surprised she'd been able to get that sentence out without choking on it. "Really?" was all he replied.

She cleared her throat and turned toward the parlor doors. "Is Aunt Penelope in her dressing room?" she asked her uncle.

"Your aunt won't be gettin' out of bed for a while yet, I'm afraid. A headache kept her up most of the night."

Rachel stopped short and looked back at the man. "How terrible," she said. But the faint smile on her lips gave away the sentiment. "I'll hurry right upstairs and check on her—"

"I've been instructed to inform you that *I* will be chaperonin' you on your ride with Beauregard this mornin'," her uncle stated, staring into his coffee mug. "Be ready to leave in an hour, Rachel Ann."

Rachel's smile drooped. "How generous of you," she murmured.

A morning ride with Beauregard, Scott thought dryly. *What a great way to start off the day.*

"Oh, Captain?" Thomas Clayborn said. "Would you care to join the three of us?"

Scott hesitated and glanced at Rachel, but the moment his eyes connected with hers she looked away. "Sure," he replied. "Why not. I haven't been horseback riding in years."

Thomas Clayborn gave him an odd look and then cleared his throat. "Will you need a pair of ridin' breeches?"

Breeches? "Uh," Scott said, smiling, "no thanks."

Clayborn shrugged, and then hefted his girth up from the rattan chair. "Suit yourself," he replied and turned for the parlor doors.

Rachel stared after her uncle until he'd disappeared into the parlor. She looked angry and dejected, and Scott couldn't help but wonder why the hell she was putting herself through all this. "Why don't you just tell these people that you're not interested in Beauregard Bodain?"

She turned to him with a startled look, and then let out a weary sigh. "Because it wouldn't do me any good.

My aunt is out to see Beau and I wed, and nothing short of death and destruction is going to stop her."

Married? "Hopefully it won't go that far."

"Oh, it won't. I can *assure* you of that."

He smiled at her determination. "Good."

She gave him a steady stare. "What's your interest in all this?"

"I don't like Bodain much myself."

"So?"

"So, you shouldn't have to spend time with a man you don't like, much less the rest of your life."

She arched a brow at him. "Care to convince my aunt of that?"

"Reasoning with older women isn't exactly my forte. In fact, my grandmother's likely to shoot me the next time she sees me." He'd demanded she stay in his house where he could take care of her, and then he'd skipped town for two days. Yep, he was definitely in for a slow, painful death.

"You have a grandmother?" Rachel asked in genuine surprise.

"Did you think I was hatched from an egg?"

"It's just that I never thought of a pirate having a family. I certainly hope your grandmother is a little disappointed in your dangerous choice of profession."

"She's used to it. I come from a long line of risk takers."

"Is your father a pirate?"

Scott laughed. "Not exactly. He was a policeman."

"Oh. Was?"

"He and my mother were killed in a pla— in a crash eight years ago."

"A train crash?"

"Yeah. A train crash." Actually they'd been killed in a plane crash, but Scott supposed that, since planes wouldn't be invented for quite some time, the clarification wouldn't do him much good.

"My parents are farmers."

Now it was his turn to look surprised. "Your parents are alive?"

"Of course."

"Then what the hell are you doing here?" he demanded incredulously. All this time he'd been figuring she'd lost her family and had been left with no choice but to come and live with relatives in the South.

Her jaw tightened. "I am *defecting*, Captain. The North has become corrupted with big industry and has forgotten about family values. *This* is where I belong."

He stared at her for a long moment. "And who are you trying to impress with that pretty speech?"

"Impressing *you* is certainly my very last concern!" she retorted. "*You* who have no loyalties except to yourself!"

"Ah-ah, don't forget my scurvy crew. One for all and all for one," he said, smiling tightly.

She came toward him, her eyes gleaming with malice. "You don't give a damn about this town or its fleet," she stated fiercely. "You don't even care about the lives being lost every day in this cursed war. All you care about is the *money* it's all earning you!"

"That's right, Rachel, I'm a criminal. A selfish, money-grubbing pirate. Which makes me wonder just what the hell it is about me you find so damn fascinating."

"Fascinating!" she shouted back. "You're immoral and unredeemable! Heaven knows where you learned that ridiculous song you were singing—"

Her hand flew to her mouth, and Scott smiled coolly down into her face. "Did you see anything you liked?"

She went rigid and lowered her hand. "I didn't see a

thing. I was merely walking by the pond—on the *other* side of the blackberry bushes—and I heard you singing. *That is all.*"

"So you didn't see me in my underwear?"

"You weren't wearing any under—" Her lips clamped tight, and his smile broadened. "What the devil were you doing bathing in the pond in broad daylight anyway!" she demanded abruptly. "No decent gentleman—"

"But I thought you'd already decided I wasn't a decent gentleman."

With a frustrated cry, she hit him across the chest with her flowers. Dozens of red and orange petals scattered down onto the deck. "You're insufferable!" she shouted. "Completely disgusting!"

"I'm not the one spying on unsuspecting naked people."

"And I am not going to stand here another second and listen to a word you have to say!" She spun around and headed for the parlor doors. "You're a complete villain!" she threw back at him.

"And you're a closet pervert."

With one last, piercing glare, she flounced into the parlor and Scott broke into laughter. He had no idea how long he would remain stuck in the past, but Rachel Ann Warren was certainly keeping him entertained.

9

It took Cassie almost an hour to dress Rachel in a riding habit, braid her hair, and then pin a jaunty riding hat with a scarf onto her head. It wouldn't have taken quite so long if Rachel had sat still. But she didn't want to go on this ride with Beau in the first place, and now that Captain Ramsey was tagging along it was bound to be miserable. He *knew* about her spying on him at the pond, and she wasn't sure she could bear his gloating.

She was standing on the front porch, grumbling and tugging on the front of her riding jacket, when her uncle, her "beau," and the cause of her ultimate humiliation rode up with her mount in tow. The captain was smiling at her in his usual infuriatingly charming way, Beauregard was glowering at the captain as if he'd stolen his favorite toy, and her uncle looked completely bored with the entire situation.

Her horse was brought forward and Rachel gritted her teeth when she saw the saddle chosen for her. It was an English sidesaddle, yet another Southern proclivity. She'd never ridden on one before, but then, maybe she'd fall and break her neck and spare herself the hour of misery ahead.

The stableman helped her mount. She carefully hooked her right leg over the horn, set her left foot in the stirrup, and then took her life into her hands by urging her horse forward. She hoped to set a fast pace, to discourage Beau from talking to her, and to get this ride over with as soon as possible.

Rachel couldn't help stealing glances at the captain as they all rode out of the yard. He was mounted on her uncle's best red roan, sitting tall and looking comfortable in the saddle. Lord, but he was a handsome devil, she thought bitterly. And, next to Beauregard Bodain, he was the absolute bane of her existence.

The four of them set off for Temple Mount, a tall grassy hillock a mile away. Rachel set the pace at a fast walk, and figured it would take them almost an hour to ride there and back. Several times Beau rode up next to her and tried to engage her in conversation. But she just smiled her best sweet smile at him and hurried her horse along. On the other hand, conversation abounded between her uncle and Scott Ramsey. At one point she even overheard them discussing cow manure.

They reached Temple Mount, and Rachel was surprised to find that, despite the company, she was actually enjoying herself. The morning air was crisp. The sun was warm against her face. Beauregard had taken the hint and seemed to be keeping his distance, and her uncle was doing a very good job at distracting the captain. Rachel turned her horse and headed back, hoping her luck would hold on the return trip.

But luck was a fleeting thing.

They were a mere ten minutes from home when a stableman came charging toward them across the meadow, carrying an urgent telegram for her uncle. Thomas Clayborn opened it, and broke into a wide grin as he read.

"Well, well," he finally said, turning to the captain. "That other backer I told you about has finally come through. He has deposited two thousand dollars in my account at the bank in town. It seems you shall have your money by the end of the day, Captain."

Rachel let out a gasp that drew all three men's attention. "What—what a wonderful surprise, Uncle," she said with a tremulous smile. "I'm sure the captain is very relieved."

"I'll ride for town immediately," her uncle announced. "I'm sure the three of you can make it back to the house on your own."

Panic was setting in fast as Rachel watched her uncle ride off across the meadow. It would take him thirty, perhaps forty, minutes to reach his bank and then return home at the pace he was riding. Her only hope was to sneak back into his study now, and take the money before he returned.

Completely forgetting about the other two men with her, she set her heels to her horse and it bolted forward, almost knocking her out of the saddle.

"Whoa," Scott Ramsey said, cutting in front of her. "Sitting the way you are, I don't know how you're staying in that saddle, Rachel, but if you're not careful you're going to end up breaking your neck."

"No proper lady rides astride, Captain," Beau remarked, coming up on the other side of her. "And speaking of proper, it really doesn't do for you to be calling Miss Warren by her given name."

"You'd rather I called her Joe?" the captain remarked. "Or maybe Frank?"

"*Miss Warren* will do quite nicely," Beau replied tightly. "I do declare," he added with a short laugh, "your coarse little manners really are beginning to try my patience."

"Really?" the captain said, casually. "Well how would you like to try my fist in your mouth?"

It was bad enough that they'd boxed her in, forcing her to move at a slower pace than she would have liked, but now they were going to start bickering back and forth over her? "Gentlemen," Rachel said in a low, warning voice. "We're almost home. Please, don't start this male posturing now."

The captain's expression relaxed and he looked off into the distance. Beauregard Bodain, however, completely ignored her. "Are you threatening me, Captain?" he stated. "Because I will have you know that I am a crack shot."

"More like a crack*pot*," Rachel heard the captain grumble.

"And if you insist on bothering myself and Miss Warren then I shall have no other choice but to demand an apology!" he added, his voice rising.

"*Another* apology for the good man," the captain remarked.

"And what, exactly, is that supposed to imply?" Beau demanded.

"That you're an idiot."

"Gentlemen, *please*," Rachel said, rolling her eyes.

"An idiot?" Beau cried incredulously, standing in his stirrups to look over at the captain. "Well, in my opinion, sir, you are a reprobate, a blackguard, a scurrilous bandit! What do you think of that?"

"That I should turn in my Boy Scout card?"

"And you say the most *ridiculous* things, Ramsey. There are times in which I doubt you're even speaking English."

"Would you like me to use smaller words?"

Beau let out a low growl, looking as if he were about to leap right over Rachel to get at the captain. "That is enough!" Rachel shouted as they came to the stream that fed the Clayborn pond. Time was wasting away, and she was in too much of an agitated state to listen to this squabbling.

She kicked her horse forward, intending to dash across the stream and leave both men behind. But the horse beneath her had something else entirely in mind. It decided to *jump* the stream, which wouldn't have been a problem had Rachel been seated in a normal saddle. But she wasn't, and the animal landed on the other side of the stream without her. She, on the other hand, landed *in* it. Hard.

Scott rushed forward and knelt down beside where Rachel lay unconscious in the water. "Help me get her to the bank," he called to Beauregard Bodain, who was standing a few yards away.

"These boots are Italian leather!" the man replied.

"Of course," Scott muttered, and scooped Rachel up into his arms. Her wet clothes added about twenty pounds to her limp body.

"Is . . . is she dead?" Bodain asked weakly as Scott laid her down in the grass.

Scott set his hand on Rachel's abdomen and once again felt the stiff constraints of her corset. "Christ," he swore. "Not again."

"Sh-should I ride for a doctor?" Beau stammered.

"Just help me get these wet clothes off her."

The man gasped and took a startled step back. "I beg your pardon?"

"Look, Bodain," Scott said, unbuttoning the front of Rachel's tailored green jacket. "What the lady needs is a little more air. Now, are you going to help me or not?"

"I most certainly am not going to undress Miss Warren!" The man's hand came down hard on Scott's shoulder. "And neither, sir, are you!"

Scott had had about all he was going to take. He reached back, took hold of Beauregard Bodain's right foot, and swept it out from under him. With a strangled cry, the man went sailing through the air and landed solidly on his back.

Scott then turned to Rachel. He finished with her jacket and turned his attention to the tiny buttons on the front of her shirt. Beneath that he found yet another cotton garment. He shook his head at how many layers she was wearing and hooked his fingers along the edges of what he hoped would be the final one. It tore easily down the front, and pearl buttons went flying everywhere.

He stared at the stiff, constricting corset beneath. Then he hooked his fingers along both edges, yanked, and popped the garment open, leaving Rachel lying there in nothing but a cotton camisole. He tried not to stare at the rosy tips of her breasts visible beneath her thin layer of clothing, but his mouth went dry with the effort. Her lungs filled with air, and it wasn't long before her eyelids fluttered open.

She stared groggily up at him, a look of confusion on her face. "Welcome back," he said to her.

"What . . . what happened?" she whispered, bringing her hand to her forehead.

"You fell off your horse. Do me a favor," he said, holding up her corset, "Don't wear these rib squeezers anymore."

She looked down at herself and let out a startled gasp. Throwing him an accusing look, she immediately sat up and gripped the front of her jacket together over her full breasts.

"Exactly!" Beauregard Bodain stated from the ground behind them. "I tried to stop him, Miss Warren, but he was insistent in his debauchery! Sir, I now must *demand* that you meet me on the dueling field!"

"Shut up, Beauregard," Scott replied darkly. He set aside the corset and smirked at Rachel, who was still staring at him in shock. "Despite what it seems, I do prefer my women conscious."

She glanced around the clearing. "Where's my horse?"

"It jumped the stream and kept going."

"That damn beast will be shot," Bodain stated, coming forward to stand beside Rachel. He reached down and took hold of her arm. "Come along, my dear. Your aunt will want to know about this."

Rachel rolled her eyes and let out a small groan. "Can't we just keep this between the three of us?"

"Hardly," Bodain said with a contemptuous snort as he tried to pull her up.

Scott stood, all of his attention focused on the tight grip Beauregard Bodain had on Rachel's arm. Fury was building in his body, and he clenched his jaw. "Let go of her, Bodain."

Scott didn't think he'd ever felt quite so volatile, and Beauregard Bodain had the unparalleled stupidity to ignore him—in fact, his grip seemed to tighten. "Miss Warren, we must get back to the house to tell your aunt what has happened—"

Without a second thought, Scott stepped forward and punched Beauregard Bodain in the face. Beau's head snapped sideways, and then, almost in slow motion, he fell backward and hit the ground.

"I only give a warning once," Scott said, shaking the pain out of his hand. "Live and learn."

"Excuse me?" Rachel said weakly from behind him.

Scott turned to see that she'd risen to her feet. She looked white as a ghost, and he swept her up into his arms just as her knees buckled. "I don't feel very well," she whispered, laying her head against his shoulder.

"It's just taking you a minute to recover," he reassured her. "You'll be fine once we get you back to the house and put you in some dry clothes."

He turned, cradling her in his arms, and strode toward his horse.

"Where are you going!" Bodain demanded from where he was still lying on the ground. "Don't you carry her off, you filthy pirate!"

Without answering, Scott set Rachel in his saddle and mounted up behind her. He didn't spare Bodain a glance as he turned his horse and started off toward the house. The only thing that mattered to him was the woman snuggled tightly in his arms.

10

Upon their return, Cassie took Rachel into her care, taking her upstairs and dressing her in a dry, warm gown. Then she led Rachel downstairs to the parlor to sit on the settee with a lap robe and a cup of hot chocolate.

Rachel could barely choke the liquid down. Her aunt Penelope and Harmony Bodain were in the dining room with Beauregard discussing this latest incident between her and the captain. The captain himself was detained in the study with her uncle, who had come home while Rachel was upstairs changing. Thomas Clayborn was probably, at that very moment, handing over every penny of that blasted fleet money to that blasted pirate. How in the world was she ever going to steal it now!

"Wouldn't a minded it at all myself," Mitzie Rothgate remarked. She was sitting across from Rachel in the Queen Anne chair, embroidering tiny yellow roses on a pillow sham. "That captain is a fine-lookin' man. Even if he is a pirate."

"Nothing happened, Granny Mitzie," Rachel stated over the edge of her hot chocolate mug. She'd been repeating that same line over and over again since returning to the house. But nobody seemed interested in listening.

The woman waved a wrinkled, dismissive hand. "That won't matter to Penelope."

And that was Rachel's greatest fear, that Penelope and Harmony would use this latest incident with the captain to force her into an engagement with Beau.

"You fancy the man," Granny Mitzie stated. "I can tell."

"I do not *fancy* Beauregard Bodain," Rachel replied evenly.

"Who said anything about Beauregard? I'm talkin' about that rapscallion pirate captain."

Rachel blinked in surprise. "That is certainly not the case."

"Ohhh, I know it ain't proper to think such things about a man like that." The old woman rose from the chair, her embroidery clutched in her knobby hands, and gave Rachel a wicked little smile. "But it sure is fun. And when you get as old as I am . . . you start thinkin' whatever the devil you like."

With that, the woman shuffled out of the room, leaving Rachel alone to panic. Had her uncle given the captain the money? she wondered frantically. Was her aunt going to use this mishap to make her and Beau wed? These moments of uncertainty were absolutely unbearable.

And then Penelope Clayborn walked into the parlor with Harmony Bodain at her heels. "Ah, Rachel dear, there you are," she said.

Rachel glanced beyond them, into the foyer, and saw Beauregard standing there, grinning from ear to ear. "I'll see you later, *Rachel Ann,*" Beau said, striding merrily out the front door.

Rachel slumped down on the settee, hoping that if she looked pathetic enough the two women might show her a little pity. But their grave expressions showed no mercy. "Rachel Ann," her aunt began, "Harmony and I have come to a decision about your latest indiscretion with Captain Ram—"

"Aunt Penelope," Rachel interjected desperately. "I told you that it was nothing. I fell from my horse—"

"Nothing?" the woman questioned. "Young lady, a man undressed you in broad daylight. That may be nothing to the common sensibilities of the North, but here in the South it is something entirely different."

"In *broad daylight*," Harmony repeated, followed by a loud clicking of her tongue.

"But he was only trying—"

"What he was attempting to do is not something we care to consider. Your reputation is at stake, and something must be done to rectify the matter immediately."

Of course, Rachel thought furiously. Her precious reputation. This had nothing at all to do with their diabolical plans for her and Beauregard. "Aunt Penelope, I promise you that I can withstand any scandal this might cause." What she couldn't withstand was being engaged to that pompous fool!

"And what of *my* reputation, Rachel Ann?" her aunt insisted. "What of the good name of Clayborn? If we do nothing to repair this situation the Clayborn name will be bandied about the streets behind shielded hands and amid whispered snickers. Is that what you want? To bring about the downfall of this good family?"

Absolutely! Rachel wanted to jump up and shout. But she bit the inside of her lip and kept quiet.

Her aunt took a deep, steadying breath. "Rachel Ann, we—that is Harmony and I—we have decided that you and Beauregard will be married at once."

It was too bad there weren't more witnesses because Rachel's jaw must have dropped clear to the floor. "*At once?*" she squeaked. "What happened to an engagement? A *long* engagement."

"We think it best that all pomp and circumstance be done away with—the wedding will take place tomorrow," Harmony declared, smiling.

"*Tomorrow!*" Rachel cried, leaping to her feet. Things were getting worse with each passing moment!

Her aunt looked down her long nose, and casually folded her hands against her skirt. "Please believe me, Rachel Ann, this is not the wedding we had planned for the two of you. But you and your captain friend have left us with no choice."

"*My* captain!" Rachel shrieked. "That man is *Uncle Thomas's* captain! And why am I being punished for something *he* has done!"

"Punished?" her aunt retorted, glaring ferociously. "Rachel Ann Warren, Beauregard Bodain is one of the most desirable and eligible bachelors in this humble state."

"The girl is quite lucky that my Beauregard will still have her after all this," Harmony added with a condescending nod.

It was apparent that yelling at these two ladies would get her absolutely nowhere, so Rachel decided to sit back down and try a little reasoning. "Aunt Penelope, if you'd only give me little more time. A few weeks?" *So I can pack my bags and get the hell out of here!* she added to herself.

"We've already sent word to Minister Timmons," her aunt replied. "I'll set the housemaids to work on my old wedding dress tonight, and by morning it will fit as if it were made for you."

That was it. The last and final straw. Rachel had had enough, and she began to shake her head adamantly. "Aunt Penelope, I am not getting married—"

"Of course if you choose not to go through with this wedding, I will have Cassie pack your bags and see that you're taken directly to the train station within the hour." Rachel blinked at the woman in surprise.

"You would send me away?" she asked, stunned. "Just because I refuse to marry the man of *your* choosing?"

"I would have no other choice, Rachel Ann. I cannot let you destroy this family's good name."

And so there it was. Good old family loyalty at its finest. Unfortunately, Rachel couldn't afford to be sent away until she got her hands on that damnable fleet money, and so she had no choice but to agree to what her aunt was demanding. Agree for the moment, anyway.

"We understand that you are a bit overwhelmed," Harmony Bodain added with a sweet smile.

Overwhelmed, yes. With disgust and outrage, Rachel thought bitterly.

"Marriage is always a bit frightening for any young girl," Penelope added. "Things will be fine once you and Beau have started off on the right foot, after you've had some time to get used to the idea."

"Oh, Rachel," Harmony Bodain said, clapping her hands. "My Beauregard will make you such a wonderful husband. Tomorrow is going to be such a *glorious* day!"

"Why so glorious?" Rachel's uncle asked, striding into the room.

Rachel looked up to see Scott Ramsey standing in the

parlor doorway, staring at her. This was all his fault. Every last bit of it. If he hadn't come along, her aunt would have no ammunition to use against her, and the money would already be in her hands.

She narrowed her eyes on the black cash box he was carrying and gritted her teeth. *Enjoy the money while you can, Captain. It won't be in your care for long.*

"Why, Rachel and Beau's wedding, of course," her aunt replied, as Thomas Clayborn continued across the room to the sideboard.

"Oh," he replied, obviously uninterested. "How nice."

"But she barely knows the guy," the captain blurted.

"*The guy,*" her aunt Penelope said, "as you so aptly put it, Captain, is a member of one of this state's oldest and best families. He is well schooled, well mannered, and well landed."

"But not exactly well liked," the captain stated in a not-so-kind tone.

Harmony Bodain let out a gasp and Rachel clenched her jaw in quiet fury. She was going to end up married within the *hour* if the man didn't shut his foolish mouth.

"Young man," Penelope Clayborn said in her best appalled voice. "Not a soul in this room has asked for your opinion."

"And not a soul cares to hear it," Harmony added.

Thomas Clayborn cleared his throat loudly from across the room. "Ladies—"

"And don't you chide us, Thomas," Penelope cut in. "If it weren't for this wretched man our Rachel Ann would have had a chance to get to know her betrothed *before* they were wed. But you, Captain, have made that impossible with your scandalous advances!"

Scott Ramsey didn't respond, but he did look straight at Rachel and she held his questioning stare with a frigid glare of her own. She wondered if he felt the least bit sorry for making such a mess of her life. And then he looked away—without so much as an apology.

"So when is the happy occasion?" her uncle asked, walking back to the captain with two small glasses of whiskey.

"Tomorrow," Penelope replied.

The captain's eyes widened, his hand freezing in midair as he reached for his drink. He looked back at Rachel and she arched a brow at him, her expression stating silently but clearly, "See what you've done?"

"Tomorrow?" Thomas Clayborn repeated, handing Scott Ramsey his drink. "Can you arrange everything by then?"

"We will only be inviting family and a few close friends. Harmony and I both plan to work on the invitations and have them delivered before the end of the day."

Her uncle shrugged. "It seems we're havin' a wedding tomorrow, Captain. Will you be attendin' the festivities?"

"I'm not sure," Scott Ramsey replied.

But Rachel didn't care whether the captain planned to attend the wedding or not. She wouldn't be there. And neither would that money he was holding.

The servants were altering the dress and preparing the food. They would pick the flowers first thing in the morning for maximum freshness. Now all that was left was for the bride to sneak off in the middle of the night before anyone caught on to her plans. But first she had to get her hands on ten thousand dollars of confederate money.

Rachel had decided not to let the fact that the money was now in the hands of an unscrupulous pirate discourage her. As long as it was still in the house, she had a fighting chance.

In her walk around the torch-lit garden that night, she paused to lean back against the thick trunk of an elm and stare up at the full moon. That same moon was hanging over her family's farmhouse in Ohio and she felt a sudden bout of longing for her mother's comforting voice. "One more night," she whispered into the cool evening air. "One more night."

"I'm assuming you've got something planned."

She started at the sound of Scott Ramsey's voice, and turned to see him standing in the shadows a few feet away. Determined to avoid him at all costs, as she'd managed to do since that momentous meeting in the parlor, she lifted her skirt and headed for the house.

"Are you running from me now?" he called after her.

She came to a halt, and slowly turned to glare back at him. "And why shouldn't I? Only the devil lurks around in the dark, Captain."

"Maybe I was hoping to stumble across some answers."

"What answers?"

He came toward her but she didn't give up an inch of ground, even when he stopped an arm's reach away. "Like where your backbone goes every time your aunt and uncle walk into the room."

"I *respect* my elders. Would you like me to define that word for you?"

"I've thought about that possibility," he replied. He shook his head. "It doesn't wash. I can see the malice glowing in your eyes when you look at them, Rachel."

"And you must be an expert on that look, Captain, you no doubt experience it everywhere you go."

"Stop trying to change the subject and tell me how you plan to get out of this marriage."

"And what if I told you I don't have a plan? That my limited options have been exhausted?"

"I wouldn't believe you."

"Or said that I've fallen madly in love with Beauregard over the course of the last few hours and can't wait to spend the rest of my life basking in the glow of his perfect complexion?"

"I'd believe you even less," he said, smirking.

"There's always the chance that Beau and I will be good for each other—even out each other's rough spots."

"A mile of sandpaper couldn't smooth that guy out. And I happen to like your edges just the way they are."

She gave him a frosty smile. "How sweet of you, but I don't have time for your pretty words right now. *I* have a *wedding* to prepare for."

She turned to march toward the house but he moved in front of her and blocked her way. "Why am I getting the impression that you're afraid of me all of a sudden?"

"I am *not* afraid of you! I am *infuriated* by you! You have single-handedly destroyed my life—or hadn't you noticed that, Captain?"

He hesitated, his expression sobering. "I'm sorry," he said softly.

Well, here was a surprise. She leaned closer, her fury mounting. "I beg your pardon?"

"I'm sorry I got you into this mess with Bodain. I never intended—"

"To act like a decent human being?" she stated bitterly. "To treat an unconscious lady with dignity? Well,

I'm sorry, Captain, but your apology has come a little too late, wouldn't you say!"

His jaw tensed, and a moment of silence hung in the air between them. The fire from the torches cast dancing shadows over his face and glittered golden in his brown eyes. "There's no law that says you have to marry him," he finally said, his tone as dark as the night surrounding them.

"My choice is simple, Captain. I marry Beau, or I'm sent home."

"Then go home."

She gave a short laugh. "It's not that simple."

"Why can't it be? You obviously hate it here."

"I don't understand where you could have gotten that impression—"

"Cut the act, Rachel. Whatever game you're playing with your aunt and uncle has nothing to do with me."

But it had *everything* to do with him. "Just because I've chosen to embrace their way of life," she replied stiffly, "doesn't mean I've chosen to embrace *them*."

"Their way of life? You mean the way they enslave other human beings and treat them worse than dogs? Is that what you're embracing, Rachel?"

Her eyes wavered, and she suddenly couldn't endure his heated stare. She couldn't admit that she loathed the practice of slavery and still maintain her "cover," but she certainly wasn't going to stand there and defend it.

He moved closer, and she instinctively lifted her hands to his chest to ward him off.

"I thought you weren't afraid of me," he said softly.

"I'm not." She was afraid of herself, of what she might allow him to do.

His charm was already beginning to work its magic on her. She felt the warmth of his skin through his shirt, heating her palms and making her weak. She felt the steady, heavy pounding of his heart beneath her fingertips and wondered what it would feel like mingled with hers. She remembered the magnificent curves and ridges of his broad chest, and knew a moment of dizzying desire.

"Are you trying to push me away . . . or pull me closer?"

She wanted to reply, tell him she was frightened and confused by the way he made her feel, but her mouth was too dry to utter a sound. Why, in God's name, did it have to be this man she was so attracted to? Her rate of breathing was increasing by the second—thank heavens she wasn't wearing a corset or she'd likely be crumbling at the good captain's feet any second. And then she'd be at his mercy again. The very idea made her face heat.

"You're looking a little undone, Rachel," he said softly. "You aren't wearing one of those damn corsets again, are you?" And then, as if to find out for himself, he curved his hands around her waist and pressed his thumbs lightly into the grooves above her hip bones.

Rachel caught her breath at the feel of his strong hands upon her. It felt so natural that she didn't resist when he drew her toward him. She slipped her hands up the front of his shirt, and his muscular shoulders provided a perfect grip when he lowered his mouth to hers.

She could have died in that moment and not cared. His mouth was warm and commanding, creating a wealth of sensations that began in her belly and radiated outward to her most distant nerve endings. She felt as if she were rising off the ground, floating on a cloud, and realized that he'd taken a firm grip on her bottom and was gradually lifting her tightly against him.

Her breasts crushed against his chest, and she arched

toward him, longing for more. His arms tightened around her as his tongue pressed at her lips, and she parted them eagerly, remembering well the heady feeling of his full possession of her mouth. The whole world drifted away on a tide of desire, and she twined her fingers into the back of his silky hair and melted into the moment.

"Rachel Ann!" Her aunt's voice, faint and distant, crept into the sensual fog surrounding Rachel. "Rachel Ann, are you out there!"

Scott Ramsey emitted a deep groan, that sounded suspiciously like regret, and set Rachel back on her feet. Rachel knew she should have let go of his shoulders at that point, but doubted she'd be able to balance on her own just yet.

"Your aunt's calling you," he said softly.

Finally, she let go of him and took an unsteady step back. His eyes were glowing with an intense heat, and she wondered if hers reflected the same.

"You can't leave until you tell me what you intend to do about Bodain."

She hesitated, although she knew she couldn't share her plans with him. "That's none of your concern."

He sighed and looked up at the night sky. "At least tell me you won't marry him, Rachel."

"Rachel Ann!"

Her aunt was getting more persistent, and Rachel had a feeling that if she didn't start heading toward the house soon the woman was going to come out looking for her. She was in no mood for a lecture on the dangers of wandering through darkened gardens with pirates.

"I have to go." She tried to brush past him, but he reached out and stopped her. The determined stare he gave her said that he wasn't going to allow her to leave until she answered him.

"Captain, I wouldn't marry Beauregard Bodain if he were the very last man in the whole entire world." She couldn't help but be pleased when his intense expression relaxed. "Now," she went on, "if your curiosity is satisfied, I'm being called back to the house."

He let go of her arm, and she slowly turned away. "I *am* sorry, you know," he called after her.

She paused, fighting a strong urge to turn back. She was still dazed by his passionate kiss, and wondered if that might be the reason she was suddenly feeling so charitable toward him.

"Rachel Ann Warren, answer me!"

Rachel let out an irritated sigh. "Coming, Auntie!" she shouted back. "Your apology, Captain," she said without turning, "is accepted."

But that doesn't change a thing between us, she added to herself as she hurried down the path. He was a pirate on a mission for the Confederates. And she was a Union spy whose mission it was to see that his did not succeed.

11

Scott lay stretched out on his bed in the dark, staring at the pattern the moonlight was making on the ceiling. It was almost midnight, nearly seventeen hours since the last time-portal had opened. He was wide awake.

He would have liked to think that he couldn't sleep because he was afraid the portal would come whirring along and he'd miss his ride home. But that wasn't the case at all. Once again it was thoughts of Rachel, beautiful, bewildering Rachel that had his mind so preoccupied.

He'd been relieved to hear that she had no intention of marrying Beauregard Bodain. *Too* relieved. Which made him wonder just what he might have done if she'd told him she had every intention of becoming the man's wife. He had a strong suspicion that he would have attended the wedding and strangled the little weasel with his bare hands.

Scott laughed out loud at himself and shook his head. He was feeling proprietary toward a woman he could never have. Forget the fact that they were born over one hundred years apart, Rachel thought he was a *pirate*, for God's sake.

He thought of home, his grandmother, and hoped everything was okay, but he wasn't at all anxious to leave just yet. Considering his conflicting emotions on the subject, he figured the best thing that could happen was for that damn portal to open up right now and suck him back the hell where he belonged.

The last time it had malfunctioned it had taken them over twenty-four hours to fix it. He'd been stuck on a mountainside in 1921 Colorado, praying it wouldn't suddenly decide to snow. He had no idea how long he was going to be stranded in the year 1862, but he did know that after that kiss he and Rachel had shared in the garden, he had one hell of a long night ahead of him.

The portal would probably come for him tomorrow . . . and then he'd never see her again. Christ, why did his chest tighten at the thought of that? Why did the mere imagining of her voice make his hands shake?

He grew irritated with himself and rolled to his side on the soft mattress. This train of thought was completely useless, and was only keeping him from getting rest. If the portal came tomorrow, he would go back to where he belonged, and somehow he'd get over Rachel Warren and her bewitching green eyes.

He closed his eyes, determined to sleep, and then suddenly heard the faint, but unmistakable creak of his door opening. He cracked an eyelid, but continued to lie perfectly still as the gentle shuffle of feet across the floor whispered through his room.

Scott couldn't imagine why anybody would sneak in on him in the middle of the night. And then he made out the trim silhouette of a woman creeping up alongside his bed. There was no mistaking the gentle fragrance of her perfume, and he figured he had to be dreaming.

What possible reason could Rachel have to visit him in his bedroom at midnight? Unless . . . Unless she'd enjoyed that kiss in the garden as much as he had and thought she'd try for a little more.

His heart rate picked up just at the idea of it, and he suddenly had to fight to keep his breathing slow and even. He thought of the sensation of having her breasts crushed against him, her lithe little body molded to his, and it made him ache with the urge to lurch up from the bed and drag her down beside him.

But the last thing he wanted to do was scare her away, so he decided to bide his time and see what the lady had in mind.

The thought of what the captain might do if he woke and caught her stealing from him had easily kept Rachel awake until midnight, the time she'd decided she would make her daring attempt. But fear had no place in her mind as she crept down the hallway to his room. She would remain calm, confident, and very, very quiet.

The curtains on the French doors were still open, letting moonlight wash through the silent darkness of his room. The captain himself looked like a shadowy lump in the middle of his mattress, breathing deeply and evenly, but Rachel still used caution as she crept up beside him. Her goal was the nightstand beside his bed.

She was only a few inches from the small table when she tripped over something large and heavy lying on the floor. She let out a startled gasp and teetered precariously on one foot before managing to right herself. Then she held perfectly still in the darkness, praying to God and all the angels that she hadn't just woken up more trouble than she was prepared to deal with.

When no sound came from the bed, she peered down at the floor, at the bulky object she'd stumbled over. With careful, quiet movements, she stooped down to have a better look.

As soon as she touched the stiff, rough material, she knew it was the captain's black canvas bag. She hesitated over it, and then decided she would look here for the money before searching the night table.

She fumbled all around the bag's curved edges, feeling for snaps or buttons, but could find none. To her estimation, there weren't any buckles or ties either. The blasted thing seemed to be one solid piece. She sat back on her heels and frowned in confusion. The bag was stuffed full of things, so there certainly *had* to be some way inside it.

She reached out once more and her questing fingers stumbled upon a tiny metal lever. She twisted it, flipped it back and forth, and finally tugged on it. To her amazement it slid toward her with a faint *whirrrr*, parting the solid piece of canvas like a hot knife through butter.

The man above her sighed in his sleep, and she ducked down, waiting a moment before relaxing and returning her attention to the strange piece of luggage. Warily she fumbled for its opened edges and then carefully eased her hand inside.

There were all kinds of different shapes and textures, and she couldn't feel any one specific thing, until her fingers tangled in a piece of stiff string. She pulled her hand back out, with the string still wrapped around it, and carefully peered at the rectangular object dangling from it.

She scooted toward the moonlight glowing off the floor a few feet away, and stared at the oddest thing she'd ever seen. It fit perfectly into her hand, and was made of some strange kind of shiny substance: not exactly glass or porcelain, but certainly not metal or wood. It was shiny, and painted a bright yellow, and the heavy black string jutted out of the top like a fuse on a stick of dynamite.

Rachel used her free hand to untangle the string from her fingers, and then followed it to its end. It split into two different sections, each section becoming thinner than the first, and led to a pair of small disks, one on each end.

She fumbled with a disk for a moment, and then turned her attention back to the yellow box itself. There were two small wheels on the back. She squinted and saw that one had the word "Tuning" written beside it, and the other had the odd word "Vol." She stared at the word "Vol" and carefully turned the wheel as far as it would go to the left. She did the same to the "Tuning" wheel, and then turned the entire object over to examine the other side.

There were three square buttons along the top edge, and they too had names: "Stop," "F.Fwd.," and "Play." Play? Could this be a toy then? she wondered. Maybe something the captain had picked up on his trips to the Orient, or some other distant place? She'd heard they were making all sorts of strange things in countries across the seas, and, deciding it must be a toy, she turned her mind to wondering what on earth it did. How could a box and string be any fun at all?

Just out of curiosity she pressed the soft button on the top that read "Stop." Then she turned the "Tuning" wheel some more, and the "Vol" wheel. She was pressing a few more of the buttons when suddenly a sound, like nothing she'd ever heard before, came from the toy and cut through the fragile silence around her. She let out a terrified cry and threw the horrible thing across the room. Then she backed up, until her thighs hit against the bed behind her.

"You kids and your loud music."

Her hand flying to her pounding heart, Rachel whirled around to see the silhouette of Captain Ramsey propped up on his elbow in the bed. He shifted, reaching for the lamp on the nightstand. It flared to life, revealing his steady gaze and his smooth, bare chest.

"You should be more careful," he added casually. "You could blow out an eardrum with that thing."

"What in God's name is it?" she found the courage and the breath to ask.

"A Walkman," he replied, and rose to a sitting position on the edge of the bed.

"Is that some kind of torture device?"

"Only if you're over the age of fifty," he replied with a quick smile. He stood and walked across the floor to pick up the Walkman. "You had the volume on a little too loud." He was turning its wheels as he came back to her. Thinking he intended to use it as punishment for sneaking into his room, Rachel almost tripped over her own feet backing away.

"It's okay," he told her. "It won't hurt you."

But what was it he'd just said about blowing out eardrums? she thought, giving him a wary look. "What is it used for?"

"Entertainment."

"Then you pirates have strange ways of diverting yourselves."

"Try it," he prodded, holding it out to her.

"I've had enough of it, thank you."

He fingered one of the buttons on the top and suddenly that noise, high and grating, was coming from it again. Rachel's heart leapt into her throat, but then she realized that the noise wasn't half as loud as it had been before. She gave it a suspicious stare.

"I turned the volume down," the captain explained. "I prefer my entertainment to be a little less painful to the ears."

"And you find this noise entertaining?"

"Listen," he said, and tilted his head toward the box resting in his hand.

Rachel did as he said, only because he didn't seem to be upset at finding her snooping in his room—and she wanted to keep it that way. Then she blinked, believing she had to be losing her mind because she swore she was beginning to make out words through all that crackling and thumping.

Her curiosity was definitely getting the better of her, and she moved a little closer so she could listen more carefully. The captain took up one of the shiny black disks attached to the divided string and lifted it toward her head.

She instantly flinched away.

"You hold this to your ear so you can hear the music better."

Music? And now that he mentioned it, it did seem as if the sound was coming not from the box but from the disk itself.

"You're not afraid, are you?" he asked, clearly baiting her.

Gritting her teeth, she reached out and snatched the disk from his hand. Then she took a deep breath and slowly held it to her ear. What she heard made her go still with amazement. "It's . . . it's singing," she whispered.

The captain nodded, still smiling.

"It says . . . not to . . . to break its heart. . . . Its achy breaky heart?" She gave him a baffled look and asked frantically, "What am I supposed to do?"

"Pray he never has another hit."

She frowned at him in confusion as he took the shiny black disk away from her and pushed a button on the toy. The singing stopped instantly. "How in heaven's name does it work?"

"Batteries," he replied.

She stared down at the object in shock. The only batteries she'd ever heard of were gun batteries. "Then it *is* some sort of weapon."

"Not those kind of batteries, Rachel. It's a type of electrical current. You have heard of electricity?"

"Of course." Electricity was now said to be powering the streetlights of Paris. But she'd certainly never heard of it causing boxes to sing. "This is really too amazing. Boxes *singing*?"

"It's not all that amazing where I'm from," he said, wrapping the string tightly around the box and then putting the Walkman back inside his bag.

"You must come across all sorts of treasures like that in your travels."

He crossed his arms over his broad, bare chest. "I've seen my share of unique things. Such as you creeping into my bedroom in the middle of the night."

Rachel's heart dropped to her stomach. She'd been a fool to even hope that he wouldn't demand an explanation, even if he hadn't actually caught her red-handed with his money. She swallowed hard at his steady stare, and knew her story would have to be good.

"Would you mind telling me what you're doing in here?" he prodded.

"I tripped over the bag and it fell open," she blurted

out. It wasn't quite what he'd asked to have explained, but she was hoping to distract him from his original question.

"You tripped over it and the zipper just sort of slid open by itself?"

"The *zipper*?" she repeated.

He picked up the bag and dropped it onto the bed. Then he grabbed hold of the tiny black lever she'd found earlier and slid it up and down along a tiny set of black tracks, thus opening and closing the bag. "The zipper," he said to her again.

She blinked at yet another intriguing device and nodded. "Right. The zipper."

"So the bag magically fell open and you thought you'd rifle through my things? Or were you looking for that elusive earring?"

"Your sarcasm is uncalled for," she replied stiffly. "And, yes, I have to admit that I became mildly curious about what might be inside the bag after it fell open at my feet. It's a very unique object in and of itself."

"Unique doesn't make it fair game, Rachel. And it certainly wasn't the reason you came slinking in here in the first place."

Rachel clenched her teeth. *Damn him for being so tenacious!* she thought furiously. "I wanted to be sure you had enough blankets," she stated tightly. "It's supposed to be a chilly night, and I know my aunt wouldn't have bothered to see to your needs. I didn't intend to wake you."

Humor sparkled in his dark brown eyes, and she wondered if he knew that it was actually turning out to be a very warm night. "You came to see to my needs? Which ones, exactly?"

Realizing now the meaning behind his twisted smile,

she gave him a serious glare. "But then again a good chilly night might be exactly what you need."

She turned to go, but, as usual, he stepped into her path. "Not so fast," he said smoothly.

Recognizing the hot glimmer in his eyes, Rachel took a hasty few steps back and collided with the tall bedpost. She held out her hand to ward him off, but he continued forward until his muscular bare chest was pressing against her fingertips.

"Where's the blanket?"

Her eyes wavered. "The what?"

"If you'd come in here and found out I was cold—and I can only imagine how you hoped to discover that if you hadn't planned to wake me up—what would you have done without a blanket?"

"I . . . I would have—"

He smiled and gradually walked forward, applying enough forward pressure on her hand to bend her arm. Finally, her fingers were curved around his shoulder and she was tilting her head back to see into his eyes.

"Would you have crawled in with me and warmed me up, Rachel?" he asked seductively. She swallowed convulsively as he reached around with both hands and took hold of the bedpost behind her. "I guarantee I would have appreciated the gesture."

A spark of fire shot through Rachel's stomach as he bent toward her. She realized in the heartbeat before his mouth touched hers that her hand had slipped up and taken hold of his neck, revealing that she wanted this kiss as badly as he did. And if she had any uncertainties, they were instantly brushed away with the smooth, warm glide of his mouth over hers.

It was a dizzying kiss, one that melted her against him and left her clinging to his shoulders with both hands.

When his tongue delved into her mouth, a ragged, needful groan echoed through the room. He pulled back from her, and Rachel was shocked to realize that she had made that lusty sound.

"Don't stop," she heard herself whisper.

His muscular arms came around her and pulled her tightly against the hard wall of his chest. The earthy scent of his skin filled her nose, the hard press of his thighs against hers made her weak. His look was starkly intent, and she had one more brief glimpse into his dark, impassioned eyes before she was once again swept away by his hungry embrace.

12

He had one hand tangled in her hair and had sent the other on a scorching path beneath her robe, where his fingers were now engaged in a seductive massage of her bottom through the thin cotton of her nightgown.

Rachel was completely lost, held captive by the passion of his kiss and by his strong arms that were pulling her tightly to his powerful body. His every move seemed to caress her, entice her, leave her wanting more.

He pulled away from her mouth and buried his face in her neck, placing lingering kisses below her ear. "I want to kiss every inch of you," he whispered urgently. "Memorize every damn curve."

Which, reason dictated, she shouldn't allow. But reason was a hard thing to maintain in the face of such raw passion.

He shifted, pressing his leg between her knees, and slipping his other hand beneath her robe to take hold of her hip. His lingering lips kissed aside her nightgown in a fiery path that trailed over the top of her shoulder and down her chest. Her breasts tingled in response, creating a liquid heat in the center of her belly, and her thighs instinctively tightened around his intruding leg.

He nudged harder, higher, pressing his thigh to that private part of her where all her longings seemed to be centered, and she let out a sharp gasp at the sudden sensation. His hands glided up her ribs, coming to a heart-stopping place just below her breasts. She held her breath as he cupped them with his palms and gently tested the soft flesh with his strong fingers.

His teeth sank gently into her arched neck, and she heard him moan deeply. Her body was coming alive with sensation, and again she felt the strong nudge of his thigh between hers.

She lost herself in the moment as he began to stroke her taut nipples through the sheer cotton material of her nightgown. This new sensation was almost more than Rachel could stand, and she bit her lip to keep from crying out. She arched against his hands in a silent plea for more while resting her head back against the bedpost.

She felt the movement of her nightgown as he slowly gathered the back of it up into his fist. She felt a brush of air on her calves, her knees, her thighs . . . and then the heat of his palm as he took a solid grip on her exposed bottom.

In that startling moment, Rachel lost all sense of place and time. There was an incomparable ache building within her, centering in the union of his thigh to her womanhood, and she began to move, hoping to soothe the need.

He accommodated her. He began guiding her in a rhythmic motion that made her cry out in shock and pleasure. With both of his hands on her naked bottom, he dragged her further up his leg until her feet left the floor and she was riding him in an erotic rhythm that left her weak with desire.

She closed her eyes, nothing mattering to her but the wild dance he'd caught her up in. His hot mouth closed over one of her nipples, and he suckled her through her nightgown. She let out a moan, wanting this crazed passion between them to go on and on, yet hoping something would finally quiet the churning need within her.

But the need only sharpened, growing and spreading throughout every inch of her body.

By the time Scott had moved on to her other breast, Rachel was coming unglued. She was clinging to his shoulders, holding him to her. Something was happening inside her, something exciting and forbidden.

"Captain," she whispered. *I'm dying,* she wanted to say, but in that moment something deep within her cut loose. It felt as though she were suddenly tossed up into the sky as a rapturous spasm broke over her body, sending tiny convulsions of pleasure throbbing through her. She saw stars dancing through her mind, and believed she'd reached out to heaven and touched the moon.

"You're the most incredible woman I've ever known."

The words were whispered against her neck in a soft, breathy rasp, and Rachel's eyes instantly popped open. Her body had finally come back down to earth, and with it her sensibilities.

What in God's name had she done! She'd cavorted with a pirate, that's what she'd done! She'd completely lost her mind!

In the flash of a second she slipped out from between the bedpost and Scott Ramsey's hard, bare chest, and stared at him with a mixture of shock and outrage. "What have you done to me!" she shouted, straightening her nightgown and robe.

He scowled. "I beg your pardon?"

A flood of indignant heat filled Rachel's cheeks. How could she have fallen so easily into the enemy's arms? "You're a despicable degenerate," she hissed. "You're a filthy, despicable pirate!"

His jaw tightened, and he suddenly looked as if he might take a violent hold on her. "I doubt that's what you were thinking a few minutes ago."

Humiliation seething through her, Rachel came at him with her hand raised, intending to slap the condescension from his face, but he caught her wrist and glared down into her eyes. "There's no victim here, Rachel. Only two consenting adults."

"You bastard," she muttered as tears burned her eyes. "You seduced me and you know it!"

"One word from you and I would have stopped."

She yanked her wrist from his tight grip. "I doubt that—you apparently have no morals at all!"

"And, apparently, neither do you."

She clenched her fists, digging her nails into her palms to keep from attacking him again. "Men like you derive a great deal of satisfaction from leading young women to their ruin," she said tightly, "but it will take more than a few practiced caresses and a mouthful of sloppy kisses to bankrupt me, Captain Ramsey." She wiped the back of her hand across her mouth for effect, not letting his darkening stare stop her from trying to salvage what was left of her pride. "I suppose I should thank you, as a matter of fact. You've shown me the perfect example of the type of man I should avoid in the future!" She spun around and flew out of his room.

"And the future's full of us, sweetheart!" he shouted after her.

Not understanding what he'd meant, and not caring, Rachel ran all the way down the hall to her bedroom, shut her door, and locked it. She rested back against the solid wood, refusing to give in to the silly tears nagging at her eyes. She supposed she'd gotten what she deserved, playing with fire like that. In fact, she was very lucky the consequences hadn't been worse, which was surely what would have happened had he known why she'd been lurking about in his room.

She wiped at her eyes, determined to consider this another of life's little lessons and learn from it. Somehow, though, this lesson hurt more than all the others combined.

Scott dropped down onto the edge of his bed. From the moment he'd met her, he'd admitted that Rachel Ann Warren was beautiful. He'd soon come to find her intelligent, mysterious, determined—and now he could add *infuriating* to that list.

He'd heard of morning-after regrets, had even stumbled through a few himself, but that little tantrum she'd just thrown had to top them all—and they hadn't even made it to the bed!

She'd actually called him *despicable*. And hell, if he'd been a filthy degenerate he'd have thrown her to the bed and satisfied once and for all this insane need he seemed to have for her. Even now the arousal he'd garnered from her passionate little ride on his leg was making him damn uncomfortable. How the hell was he supposed to sleep now?

He reached for his bag and whipped open the zipper. He shuffled around past his pair of sweatpants and pad of notebook paper until he found what he was searching for.

He smiled grimly as he pulled out the "girlie" magazine with Miss May's ample bosom plastered all over the cover.

He stretched out on the bed and cracked the magazine open to the centerfold. Then he settled his eyes on the sleek, curvy body of the model.

He thought of kissing those shiny red lips, but ended up envisioning running his tongue over a full, natural-pink mouth. Grunting in irritation, he turned his attention to Miss May's abundant, pale breasts. He envisioned licking those dark, dusky nipples, but soon his mind had turned to kissing a pair of perfect hand-sized breasts with rigid little pink nipples that tightened at his slightest touch.

"Damn it!" he swore. She was torturing him even in the presence of a voluptuous, naked sex object!

He tossed the magazine aside and closed his eyes. Rachel Ann Warren was hell on wheels, and he would *not* let her get to him like this. He'd been stupid to let things go as far as they had between them; this attraction he felt for her was pointless. Chances were the time-portal would come for him first thing in the morning. He'd get up bright and early and head for the meadow. And between now and then he wouldn't give Rachel Warren another thought.

It took Scott quite some time to fall asleep that night. And when he finally did, his dreams were filled with Rachel and her flashing green eyes.

13

With very little sleep to sustain her through what was bound to be a frantic day, Rachel left her bedroom early the next morning to fetch a cup of coffee from the kitchen. She may have failed in her attempt to steal the money from the captain, but she would *not* fail in cajoling, cheating, *beating* it out of him before the morning was over.

After all the bragging she'd done to her brothers about finding that money, she'd never be able to hold her head up again if she failed now. She would get the cash and make her escape before the first wedding guest arrived.

She was yawning and rubbing the sleep from her eyes, shuffling along the carpet runner toward the stairs, when a familiar voice made her stop cold. "Prewedding jitters keeping you awake?"

The remark had been nothing short of snide. The good captain was lucky all Rachel was capable of giving back was a vicious scowl. "I had a rather *nauseating* night, and I thought I'd get something from the kitchen to settle my stomach."

"Overexertion can do that to you," he replied with a cool twist of his lips.

"So does wallowing in filth."

"And you did your share of wallowing last night, didn't you?"

Despite her anger, Rachel felt a hot blush creep up her neck. She was clenching her teeth so hard her jaw was starting to ache. Then she noticed the black bag in the captain's hand, and, unable to curb the alarm in her voice, she demanded, "Where are you going?"

"Afraid I'll miss the ceremony?"

"There's not going to *be* any ceremony," she replied.

"Beauregard Bodain should appreciate his narrow escape," the captain muttered as he began to descend the stairs.

Rachel hurried toward the banister, her eyes still on that black bag; he could be walking out the door for good, and taking her last hope with him. "You *will* be here for the ceremony, won't you?"

He paused halfway down the staircase, and looked back at her. She expected to receive another cool glare, and so the heat radiating from his brown eyes surprised her. He took in every inch of her body as she stood there clad in nothing but her nightgown and robe. Although he was half a staircase away, she still felt that hungry stare as if he'd reached out and touched her. In response, her stomach took a dive toward her toes.

Finally, he looked away and continued down the rest of the stairs. "Have yourself a nice life, Rachel Ann Warren."

Rachel stood there staring in disbelief as he walked out the front door and closed it behind him. He'd left.

Just like that. After he'd seduced her into a molten ball of fire the night before all she had gotten was a "have yourself a nice life!"

She gripped the banister, torn between bursting into tears and screaming at the top of her lungs. It was gone. Every penny. After she'd spent two torturous weeks trying to find it, he'd packed it up in his little black bag and sauntered out the door with it! And the worst part was, she was going to miss him! She was going to miss that despicable, *infuriating* pirate!

Taking a long, deep breath, Rachel got hold of her emotions. It certainly wasn't over. That money was fair game until it sailed out of her reach. And that absolutely was *not* going to happen.

"We're not finished yet, Captain," she said. "Not by a long shot."

She turned and marched back to her room, determined to dress and ride out after him. However, the last thing Rachel expected when she threw open her bedroom door was to be met by the indomitable scowl of her aunt Penelope.

"What are you doing lurking about the house at this hour of the morning?" the woman demanded.

Rachel's first instinct was to stammer out a humble excuse, but then she realized that she didn't have to be nice to her disdainful aunt anymore; the money was no longer in the woman's house. "I needed a cup of coffee."

"You weren't off cavorting with the servants again, were you?"

"Of course," Rachel replied flippantly, heading for the armoire. "I thought, what the hell, one last fling."

Penelope Clayborn's responding gasp could have toppled a tree. "*I beg your pardon?*"

Rachel opened the doors on the armoire, took out her

gray skirt and white ruffled shirt, and tossed them across the back of a chair. She hoped there would be somebody awake at the stable to help her saddle a horse.

"Young lady, what are you doing?"

"Getting dressed," Rachel replied, walking toward the dresser to retrieve a pair of pantalets and stockings from the top drawer.

"That is certainly *not* what you are wearing to your wedding. Cassie will be bringing your gown along shortly—"

"There isn't going to be a wedding."

The room fell silent except for the soft rustle of material as Rachel slipped her underdrawers on beneath her nightgown. "I thought we discussed this matter yesterday, Rachel Ann," her aunt finally replied in a stern voice. "This fit of nerves is perfectly nor—"

"This isn't a fit of nerves!" Rachel snapped, and Penelope flinched back in surprise. "This is *me* telling *you* no, Aunt Penelope. *No!*"

The woman's eyes hardened as Rachel slipped off her robe and nightgown. "Where is this disgraceful behavior coming from?"

She gave her aunt a sardonic smile and held out her arms. "From me, Aunt Penelope. From plain old me."

"It's that pirate, isn't it? He's finally managed to corrupt you!"

"The pirate," Rachel stated bitterly, pulling on her shirt, "is gone. As I will be in just a few short minutes."

"You're running off with him! Rachel Ann, surely you must realize how foolish—"

"*Foolish* is the idea of me marrying that pasty-faced imbecile!"

There was a tense moment as Rachel stepped into her skirt and then buttoned the back. She sat down in the chair to slip on her stockings, her mind on the road she would have to race down in order to catch up with Captain Ramsey. "I cannot let you do this, Rachel Ann."

She gave the woman a cursory glance and reached for her shoes. "You have no say in the matter."

"Oh, but I'm afraid I do. I am still the mistress here, still your aunt, your guardian, and I am telling you that I will not let you leave this house to go chasing after that nefarious scoundrel."

A gentle knock came at her door, and Cassie poked her head into the room. "I brung the dress, Missus Penelope."

"It isn't needed," Rachel stated.

"Bring it in, Cassie," Penelope said, glaring at Rachel. "I know that Miss Rachel is just going to love it."

Cassie stepped into the room carrying a satin and lace wedding gown with seed pearls sewn in a rose design on the bodice. Rachel clutched her shoes and glowered at the dress. "I am *not* getting married," she said once more.

"You are," her aunt replied. "It's bad enough that I've had to put up with your coarse Northern manners, but I will not have you running off now and disgracing me and this family."

Rachel stood slowly from her chair. "And how do you propose to get me into that dress, *Auntie*?"

Her aunt pursed her lips and turned to the shocked maid still holding the gown. "Cassie. I want her in that dress and looking perfect within the hour. Or *you* will pay the price for it."

Rachel let out a gasp as Penelope turned for the door. "You vicious, old—"

"This wedding shall be absolutely flawless, Rachel Ann," her aunt paused to say. "And just in case you get it into your head to try and sneak out of the house to become that pirate's floozie, I will have a man posted at the foot of the staircase."

Penelope Clayborn left the room, quietly closing the door behind her, and Rachel dropped back down into the chair. Her aunt was actually going to hold her prisoner until she could hand her over to Beauregard Bodain. When was this nightmare going to end?

The narrow-skirted wedding gown was a perfect fit, making it doubly hard for Rachel to dash down the long hallway from her room to the one previously occupied by Scott Ramsey. Her wedding was in less than an hour. With a man posted at the bottom of the stairs to prevent her from leaving the house, her only hope for escape was a truly daring one.

She barged into the bedroom, shut the door, and locked it. Then she took a moment to take a deep breath—she'd convinced Cassie to forgo the corset; she was going to need all the air she could get to execute her plan. Her aunt had poked her head into her room a few minutes before, and had proclaimed Cassie's efforts a glowing success, so the poor maid was now off the hook. It was too bad Rachel couldn't yet say that for herself.

She looked across the room to the French doors that led out to the veranda. "Please, God, don't let me break my neck now," she whispered. She started across the floor, but what she saw resting beside the bed on the night table brought her to a complete halt. It was the cash box.

Her throat tightened, and she squeezed her eyes shut, wondering if she had any hopes of catching up to

Captain Ramsey now that he had over two hours' head start on her. She glanced at the bed, remembering the passionate moments they'd shared the night before, and felt tears burn her eyes. She stared down at the cash box, and, rediscovering her bitterness, she reached for it with both hands, intending to throw it across the room. But the black metal box was heavier than it looked, and when she lifted it, she felt something shift inside even though she was sure it was empty. Her heart nearly leapt into her throat.

She sat down on the edge of the bed, cradling the box in her lap, and closed her eyes in prayer. "Please, God," she whispered. "Not for my pride, but for all the lives that will be saved." Then slowly, she cracked open the lid, and opened her eyes.

A muffled sob rose from her chest and she lifted her hand to her mouth. The money was there. Ten thousand dollars worth of confederate bills.

She reached in and touched a stack with reverent fingers, still unable to believe her own eyes. A laugh slipped out from between her lips. She'd been waiting for this moment for so long that it almost seemed unreal.

Then her eyes wandered to the fireplace across the room. Her brothers had told her to get rid of the money the instant she found it, so, with determination, she stood and walked across the floor.

She emptied the contents of the box onto the grate. Regrettably she couldn't turn around and offer the money to the Federal forces. The Confederate States of America were not recognized as a separate country, thus neither was their currency. She took a match out of the match safe on the wall, and then bent down and set fire to the whole mess. She smiled as she watched it all go up in a bright red flame and a few puffs of smoke. There would be no Glennville fleet. There would be no arms to subsidize the Rebel revolt. Thus the war would end that much sooner.

She'd done it, although not without a few calamities along the way. Her thoughts turned back to Scott Ramsey. Why on earth had he left the money behind? That he'd forgotten it seemed to be the only explanation. Which meant he could be coming back for it at any moment.

Her gaze shot in the direction of the veranda. The morning sunshine was glowing bright and hot through the windowpanes. She walked forward and opened the French doors, then walked out to the railing and stared down at the lawn more than twenty feet beneath her. She was going to break her neck.

She had no other alternative but to take the chance. If she stayed any longer she would be married to Beauregard, and at this point that wasn't even the worst of it: If anyone discovered that she'd destroyed the fleet money, she could quite possibly hang.

Rachel hiked her dress up past her knees and climbed up onto the wide railing. There was a tall, sturdy oak growing only a few inches away from the veranda, and she reached for the thick branch above her head. Then she set her foot on a lower branch and edged out toward the trunk of the tree. It was a slow, methodical climb downward, and she barely took a breath until her feet were resting on solid ground once again.

She wasted no time in hurrying to a hidden place behind the tall shrubs alongside the house. There was a back path that led to the pond. It was rarely used, and badly overgrown, but she knew it was her best hope of slipping away without being seen.

She crept to the corner of the house and peered around toward the front entrance. Her breath caught and she quickly ducked back when she saw her uncle standing on the front walk with four other men. "I'm sure there's an explanation for all of this," he was saying.

Rachel peeked again and saw Charles and Beauregard Bodain, dressed up in gray tuxedos. Next to them was Harold Trolley. But Rachel wasn't sure who the fourth was—a straggly looking stranger.

"I knew that captain was a bounder the moment I set eyes on him!" Beauregard stated furiously. "You should have thrown him out on his ear the moment he looked sideways at your niece!"

"Quiet, Beauregard," Charles Bodain snapped. "He had us all fooled."

Frowning, Rachel listened harder.

"Where exactly did you say you found this man?" her uncle demanded, pointing at the gentleman she didn't recognize.

"On the road just outside of Glennville," Harold Trolley answered stiffly. "Our first blasted assumption was right, Thomas. Captain Remsby has been stalled this past week by the damned blockade."

Captain *Remsby*? Rachel thought, peering harder at the scurrilous-looking man.

"Ramsey was obviously working for the Yankees!" Beauregard blustered. His face was turning redder by the second. "We've all heard the rumors of them sending someone to thwart our plans!"

Her uncle scowled heavily. "If Ramsey is a spy, then I'll shoot the man myself."

Rachel's heart nearly stopped. Captain Ramsey? A spy? "How do we know *this* man is who he says he is?" Charles Bodain demanded.

"I don't have ta prove myself to you," the straggly man growled. "Either ye want ships, or ye don't!"

Now this man definitely looked like a pirate, Rachel thought to herself, with his long, stringy hair, and his thick mangy beard. He was gigantic in size, and looked as if he could—and would—eat an entire human being for breakfast.

"What about the money, Thomas?" Harold Trolley asked.

There was a moment's pause, and then her uncle replied, "I gave it to him last night."

"Which was why he was in such a hurry to leave this morning," Charles Bodain replied.

"Are ye tellin' me ye don't have me money?" the pirate demanded.

"We'll get your money back, Remsby. Make no mistake about that."

"I say we gather some men and hunt Ramsey down!" Beauregard shouted.

"Young man, your weddin' is in thirty minutes," her uncle retorted. "I'll not have my wife haranguin' me for the rest of my life if this matter interferes with that. There is only one road leadin' from here to Savannah. We'll gather some men *after* the ceremony, and hunt Ramsey all the way to the Atlantic if need be."

The men started filing into the house. "Can't wait to get that villain in my shotgun sights," Harold Trolley said.

"Dirty Yankee spy," Charles Bodain grumbled.

Rachel waited until the front door closed behind them before edging out into the open. Her mind was working a mile a minute as she hurried toward the overgrown path. If Scott Ramsey wasn't the captain her uncle had contacted, then who the devil was he?

He surely couldn't be a spy as they were all suggesting. Her brothers would have warned her if someone else were on the job.

And then she remembered how much Jeremy and Zach had always doubted her ability to find the money. What if they'd installed a backup plan without telling her, had enlisted one of their soldier friends to sneak in on the sly?

Her jaw tightened as she reminded herself that Scott Ramsey had left that cash box right out in the open, almost as if he were taunting her with the fact that he had beaten her to the punch.

"Damn them," she whispered furiously, striding down the path. "Damn all three of them!"

14

Scott leaned back against the tree behind him and shaded his eyes with his hand. He'd been waiting in the meadow for over two hours now, and there was still no sign of the time-portal. In fact, he was beginning to get a little nervous. What if something had really gotten screwed up, and he was stuck in the past forever? What would happen to his grandmother? He'd been gone for three days, and he certainly hoped Tayback had been sending somebody to his house regularly to check on her.

Some women certainly needed him more than others, he thought caustically, his thoughts inexplicably turning back to Rachel. And to think he'd actually started to believe she might like him just a little bit. But she'd pretty much dispelled that thought the night before.

The woman despised him, plain and simple, and for some reason he just couldn't get over it—or her. It was driving him *crazy* that he was about to step out of her life forever, and he hated to think how hard it would have been if they'd actually made love the night before.

He heard a sound behind him, and turned to look. What he saw nearly took his breath away. It was Rachel, coming toward him down an old, overgrown path. And in a wedding dress, no less.

"Well," she stated, seeing him at almost the same moment he saw her. "Look who we have here."

He couldn't help smiling up at her as she marched toward him. "I expected you to be in the middle of backing out of a wedding about now," he replied.

"And I expected you to be miles and miles away," she said with a cool little smile. She crossed her arms and glared down at him. "But, maybe now I can get a few straight answers."

He stood and brushed the grass and leaves off his jeans. "And what answers would those be?"

"Let's start with an easy one. Who are you and what are you doing here?"

He frowned and glanced around the meadow. "Haven't we done all this once before?"

"This time I expect the truth, Captain Ramsey. *If* that's your real name."

"Of course that's my real name. What the hell is this about?"

"It's about mistrust. It's about betrayal. It's about a bunch of arrogant men who couldn't leave well enough alone!"

Scott stared at her, and then shook his head. "I have absolutely no idea what you're talking about."

"Of course you don't," she replied sarcastically. "I never thought for a moment you'd admit your scheme to me. But I have news for you, *Captain Scott Ramsey*. I overheard a conversation between my uncle and a few of his friends earlier. . . ." She paused dramatically and squinted up at the bright sky. "It seems that as Harold

Trolley was riding through town today on his way to my spectacle of a wedding he picked up a passenger. A man by the name of *Remsby*."

"Remsby?"

"*Captain* Remsby. And, unlike you, the man looks *remarkably* like a pirate."

Realization dawned, and Scott finally understood why she was so infuriated with him. It was time to cut his losses. "I never said I was a pirate, Rachel."

"But you certainly led us all to believe that's what you were, didn't you!" she shouted back. "All that talk about traveling to China—"

"I *have* been to China."

"Allowing all of us to go on calling you Captain—"

"I *am* a goddamn captain!" He sighed, and gave her a steady stare. "Look, I'm not the one who introduced me to her uncle as some pirate out to run a blockade."

"Don't you *dare* blame this on me! You were perfectly capable of voicing your identity at any time during the past three days, but you were too intent on making a fool out of me!"

"As if you ever needed any help," he grumbled.

She stepped forward and jabbed him in the chest with her finger. "*You* are even more despicable than I thought you were, *Captain Scott Ramsey!* And at least when you were a pirate you had an excuse!"

"Stop saying my name like that—I *am* Captain Scott Ramsey."

She gave him a cool stare. "A captain in the *Confederate* navy?"

"Not exactly." *Oh, and by the way,* he added to himself, *my ships sail through the air, not the water.*

She smirked at him, as if he'd just confirmed her suspicions. "I wonder how they'll feel when I tell them you seduced me, Captain. I wouldn't put it past them to shoot you, friend or not."

"What the *hell* are you talking about!" he bellowed. The woman seemed bent on sending him over the edge!

She gave him an innocent stare. "Keep your cool, now. That's the first rule of being a spy."

"So now you think I'm a spy?" He let go with a sardonic laugh. "Oh, this just keeps getting better and better."

"They should have told me," she blurted. "Better yet, they should have *trusted* me!"

"*They*?" he asked, but she'd turned and started walking off toward the pond a few yards away. So he picked up his bag and followed her.

"If you value your life, I suggest you find yourself a good place to hide, Captain. They'll be looking for you soon—and I would forget about trying to take the road to Savannah."

"Who the hell is *they*?" he demanded once again.

"Uncle Thomas, Harold Trolley, the Bodains. They know you're a Union spy and are intent on shooting you."

Shooting him? "Goddamn it, Rachel, I am *not* a spy!"

"That's very good," she replied, shoving a vine out of her way as she skirted the blackberry bushes. "But if you enunciate the word '*spy*' when you try that denial on them, it might make the lie a little more convincing."

He clenched his jaw at her stubbornness, and then realized that the trail they were on led in the opposite direction from the house. "Where are you going?" he demanded.

"To a safe hiding place. And you?"

"Then you *did* back out on the wedding?"

"I think that's rather obvious."

And now she was hiding? "I assume your aunt didn't take it well?"

"That's putting it mildly."

"And now you're running?"

"Very good, Captain. Bravo."

"What will they do if they catch you?" If she needed him to stay and help her escape, he would.

She paused on the narrow path and looked back at him. "They won't catch me. Are you planning on following me the entire way?"

"That depends on where you're going."

"I told you, to a safe hiding place."

Yep. She was definitely going to need him to stick around for a little while. "Then considering I'm a walking target at the moment, I guess it would make sense for me to stay with you."

She gave him a considering look, her green eyes glittering in the sunshine. "Then hurry up, and keep your voice down," she finally said, turning back to the path. "I've worked too hard to let it all end now."

Deciding now was not the time to question her about what she meant by that, Scott settled his eyes on the twitch of her narrow, white satin skirt, and followed along behind her. He'd gone from being a time-traveler to being a scurvy pirate to being a Union spy, and all during the course of just a few short days. No wonder he was so damn tired.

The dirt and sharp branches were systematically destroying her aunt's ivory satin wedding dress. The path was almost completely overgrown with clinging kudzu vines and blackberry bushes, but that would certainly work in their favor once the search parties began looking for them.

Rachel wasn't sure why she was being so generous

and letting Scott Ramsey follow her. She assumed it probably had something to do with Union loyalty, and nothing at all to do with the way her stomach turned when she thought about her uncle and his friends getting their hands on him.

"I guess I should thank you for helping me get away," he called to her.

"I happen to find shootings very unsavory, Captain. But I hear they're kinder than hangings," she added, skirting in between two close-growing trees.

"I'll try to keep that in mind."

She caught the heel of her white shoe in a rock hole and stumbled slightly. He reached out and steadied her, and she mumbled a thank you before quickly stepping ahead of him again. He hadn't touched her since the night before, but her body had definitely not forgotten how to react, and she took a deep breath to rid herself of the momentary weakness.

"There's supposed to be an old hunting lodge a few miles up this path," she told him. "It's hidden within the trees."

"I hope you intend to go home after all this," he said out of the blue.

"And where else would I go?"

"Then you do plan to leave the South?"

"I hate it here," she replied, loving the liberating feeling of finally being able to say that out loud. "I can't wait to get back to Ohio." Her parents were going to be so proud to learn that she'd accomplished her mission. "Tell me something, Captain," she added. "Why did you leave the money on the nightstand?"

"*You* found it?"

Well he certainly didn't have to sound so surprised. "Of course I found it," she retorted.

"I left it there because it wasn't mine."

Damn right it wasn't his. She'd spent two miserable weeks at that house searching for that money. "And what if I hadn't discovered it this morning?" she asked tightly.

"Then your uncle would have found it."

Rachel clenched her jaw. He'd been handed the money—practically on a silver platter—and then left it, and it would have been all her fault if she'd somehow overlooked it? She was going to box her brothers' ears when they came for her later that night.

"Will you be catching a train heading north?" he asked.

"A train?" She lifted the front of her dress and stepped up onto the fallen tree where she normally met her brothers.

"To Ohio."

He offered her his hand, to help her get down the other side, and she took it without thinking. The touch of his fingers caused a disconcerting tingle up her arm. She hopped down to the ground and quickly snatched her hand back. "I'm not sure how I'm getting home," she answered.

"Doesn't sound like much of a plan."

"It's apparently better than the one you had," she snapped. If not for her, he probably would have been captured by now. "What were you waiting for, any-way?"

"When?"

"In the meadow. You could have had a good three- or four-hour head start on them if you'd hurried."

"I was waiting for my ride," he replied rather dryly.

"And what happened?"

"It never showed."

She frowned, knowing that probably meant his contact had either been stopped for questioning or captured. "I certainly hope everything is all right."

"So do I, Rachel. . . . So do I."

They walked on down the rocky path, over a stream, and through thick patches of bracket ferns. The sun was barely filtering through the heavy overgrowth of trees and soon the trail turned slick and muddy.

"Watch your step," he said from behind her as they trudged through a particularly wet spot.

"You watch yours. I won't be able to carry you if you slip and break your leg."

"And if I did, would you leave me lying out here for your uncle to find?"

There was a teasing note in his voice, and she glanced back and found him smiling at her. "I suggest you do your best not to give me the option," she replied, trying her best to look threatening.

"I thought you shuddered at the thought of a shooting."

"I am helping you out of the goodness of my heart, Captain. Don't make me regret it."

"So then you admit your heart's involved?"

She stopped and turned to glare back at him. "What kind of question is that?"

"I was just wondering if maybe it's *my* shooting in particular that you're trying to avoid."

His statement was a little too close to the mark for Rachel's comfort, so she rolled her eyes and turned away from him. "Has it occurred to you, Captain, that I might be helping you in order to save my own neck?" She lifted the already filthy hem of her dress and stepped over a thick mud puddle. "For all I know you might have tried turning me in to them in order to save yourself."

She let out a small cry as he took her by the arm and

spun her around to face him. "You couldn't think me capable of something so despicable," he demanded, his dark eyes intense.

He was right. It had been a hateful thing to say, and an apology was wavering on the tip of Rachel's tongue. But she couldn't quite swallow her pride long enough to offer it. "We have to keep moving," she said, her voice trembling slightly.

"What will they do if they catch you helping me?"

She found she couldn't meet his eyes, so she focused on the grip he still had on her arm. "They'll probably shoot us both, Captain. The fact that I'm Thomas Clayborn's niece won't matter in the slightest."

His grip slackened, and then he let go of her to brush his fingertips along the underside of her jaw. A wave of longing coursed through Rachel and she felt her cheeks go hot.

"We . . . we shouldn't be stopping," she said, her voice no more than a whisper. The lodge . . ." Her words faded off as his thumb glided over her bottom lip.

"The lodge?"

"The lodge should be just ahead," she finished quickly, before her voice deserted her again.

A look of regret slipped over his face, and his warm hand fell away. He gestured toward the path. "Lead the way, Pocahontas."

Rachel turned and began walking again, this time with a new weakness in her legs.

"How do you know about this lodge, anyway?" he asked after a few quiet moments.

"My brothers told me about it."

"Your brothers?" he replied, sounding surprised.

"They stumbled on it last week, and decided it would be an ideal place for me to hide. I certainly couldn't steal the fleet money and then wait around for them to come riding up to rescue me."

"Stop!"

Startled by the captain's shout, Rachel came to an immediate halt, and whirled around to face him. She almost expected to see him surrounded by shotguns, but he was simply standing there, looking quietly furious.

"I am *sick* of feeling as if you're talking circles around me," he stated flatly. "Now. Very slowly. Explain what you just said."

"About my brothers?" she asked carefully.

"And them riding up to *rescue* you?"

"Yes."

"After?"

"After I'd stolen the fleet money—I don't see why this is so complicated—"

He held up his hand and gave her a tight smile. "Humor me for a minute. You'd planned to *steal* the fleet money?"

"Of course. Don't tell me you're now going to deny knowing about that."

He closed his eyes for a brief moment, looking as if he were desperately trying to remain in control. "Why?"

"*Why?* Because that's what I was sent here to do."

"Sent by who?" he asked evenly.

His intense stare was really starting to unnerve her, and Rachel laughed, albeit nervously. "Don't be absurd—"

"*Sent by who!*"

"By the Union, of course!" she shouted back. His mouth dropped open and he went white as a sheet, and if Rachel hadn't recently realized what a proficient actor he was, she would have been alarmed. "You're . . . you're a *spy*?" he asked, sounding incredulous.

Rachel's certainty about who he was wavered for a moment, but then she shoved her doubts aside. "Really, Captain," she replied, turning back to the path. "Your continued act of ignorance is really beginning to annoy me."

15

"Act of ignorance!" Scott fired back at her. "How the hell was I supposed to know that *you* were a Union spy!"

Rachel turned back to Scott, and he looked at this amazing woman in a whole new light. She was dressed in a mud-splattered, satin wedding dress that hugged her small waist and full breasts like a second skin, making him want to take a slow, exploratory trip from one end of her to the other. Her hair was a mass of dark curls, some hanging loose and clinging to the sides of her neck, and the rest pinned on top of her head in a sexy, tangled style. She looked like a battered fairy princess. But Rachel Ann Warren was a *Union spy*.

"How could I have known?" he repeated, still flabbergasted.

"Because you were sent here to check up on me, that's how," she retorted.

"Rachel," he said tightly, and for what had to be the tenth time. *"I* am not a spy."

She rolled her beautiful green eyes at him. "Of course you're not."

Scott stared after her as she turned and continued up the path, thinking that would have been a very nice thing to finally hear her say—if she'd meant it. "So," he called, following behind her. "How long have you been in the spy business?"

"This is my first mission."

"And can I assume your last?"

"I haven't decided that yet, Captain."

That hadn't been the answer Scott wanted to hear. "Isn't it a little dangerous, Rachel?"

"No more dangerous for me than anybody else. Maybe even less, in fact. Men tend to doubt that a woman is *capable* of spying on them."

That wasn't exactly true in Scott's experience. When it came to finding out certain aspects of his life, such as whom he was dating and when, his grandmother was probably the best covert operations expert he'd ever met.

Rachel reached up to hold back a tree branch, and then faltered at something she saw off to her right. She turned and pushed aside some heavy vines from the wall of foliage lining the trail, and Scott stepped up beside her to have a look for himself.

"I think we found it," she said.

Scott pressed back some prickly blackberry branches and peered through the thick vegetation. Although the log outline was well hidden within the tight-knit trees, he could definitely see some sort of cabin a few yards away.

"Do you see it?" she asked.

"I see it."

He turned sideways, reached through the scratchy branches, and tossed his bag to the other side. Then he slid through himself, careful not to disturb too much of the natural camouflage. He could see the cabin better now, nestled in a little clearing, and he turned to help Rachel. "Careful," he warned, holding tightly to her hand.

Once she was through, he rearranged the brush to cover their passage, and then walked forward with her toward their precarious shelter. "Do you think it's stable?" she asked softly, stopping beside him in front of the broken stoop.

It sure as hell didn't look that way to him. He watched her nudge the outside wall with the toe of her muddy white shoe, and a clod of dirt and grass fell from the crack between the logs. The open front door was hanging from one hinge. The front window was broken out, and the roof looked as if it might not be completely intact. And, Scott thought grimly as a mouse nosed its way around the entrance, he had a feeling they wouldn't be the only guests.

"Only one way to find out." He picked up his bag and walked forward to peek around the doorway. The place was definitely a mess. What was left of the furniture was in broken shambles, lying in the corner—probably meant for firewood, and there was a layer of dirt as thick as the Sahara covering the floor.

He looked up, and was surprised to see that the roof was basically in one piece. There was a large hole toward the far side of the timber ceiling, but he didn't see that as any problem compared to the state of the rest of the place.

He gave the doorjamb a good shake. "It seems pretty sturdy," he said. A garter snake went slithering across the filthy floor, and he figured he'd better go in and scare off some of the current proprietors before Rachel went inside. "Wait out here while I take a look around."

"Forget it, Captain. I intended to come here alone, remember? And the last thing I want or need is you coddling me."

Scott shrugged. So much for chivalry.

He stepped inside the cabin and the floorboards beneath his feet creaked loudly, creating an eerie feeling that made his spine tingle. Rachel was staying right beside him. She was standing so close, in fact, that their hips were brushing. Brave or not, he knew this place had to be giving her the creeps, and he fought the urge to put his arm around her.

"Not very homey, is it," he remarked.

"I'm sure that's why my brothers chose it," she answered softly. "It's obviously been deserted for quite some time."

A soft shuffling sound came from the other side of the darkened room and she pressed a little closer to him. "You don't think there are any wild animals in here, do you?"

Scott smiled into the darkness. "Looks like a perfect bear hangout to me."

There was a moment of silence, and then she asked, "Bears don't eat people . . . do they?"

"They can give it a good try."

Another noise came from across the room. Rachel let out a muffled cry and scooted behind his back. "What was that?"

"An awfully small bear," he replied, unzipping his bag. He fished around among his belongings for a moment, until he found the nine-volt flashlight. Then he set his bag down on the floor, and flicked it on.

The entire one-room cabin lit up in a muted white light, and Rachel just about went through the ceiling. "What's that!" she shouted, while trying desperately to merge with his spine.

Sorry that he hadn't realized how shocked she'd be by something so strange to her, Scott reached back and put his arm around her slender shoulders. "It's all right," he said, pulling her close. "It's just a fancy lantern."

She stared at the flashlight, and reached out to run her fingers over the smooth plastic. "Where did you get it?" she said, obviously amazed by the lack of a flame.

"Circuit City." He pointed the broad beam of light in the direction of the sound and saw a small pair of golden eyes glowing at them. "Psst!" he said. He stamped his foot, raising a cloud of dust, and the raccoon scampered out through a hole in the side of the wall.

"Is that in England?"

"Is what in England?"

"Circuit . . . City."

Scott chuckled. "It might be."

She gave him an odd look and then smiled, and he was instantly caught in the magnificent depths of her pale green eyes. His body began to react to the soft press of hers against his side, and he found himself entranced by the gentle curve of her lips. Before he knew it, his head was moving down toward hers, and he was anticipating the taste of her mouth.

She lurched away from him as if he'd set her hair on fire. "There's, um, there's supposed to be a bedroll and some supplies waiting for me around here somewhere."

Good going, Ramsey, Scott thought to himself. Just when she was beginning to let him get a little closer he'd had to go and push his damn luck.

He turned the beam of the flashlight to the back of the room and saw what looked like a cot against the far wall. There was a bulky shape resting on it, and he walked across the room to check it out. It turned out to be a roll of blankets, and a small satchel with some clothes in it.

"I think I found your supplies," he called to Rachel, who'd remained in the light of the doorway.

She hurried forward. "Is there a change of clothes?"

He held up the satchel. "One change of clothes, coming up."

"Thank heavens," she said, sighing gratefully. "I was afraid I was going to have to wear this dress all the way home . . . to . . . Ohio."

The falter in her voice came as she saw his reaction to the news that she intended to change her clothes. He couldn't help the surge of heat that had raced through his body at the thought of it, or the intent look he'd given her. Did she actually plan to strip down right there in the cabin with him standing just a few feet away? Christ, the thought of it had his heart pounding like a conga drum.

He turned and walked back toward the door, searching for something to occupy his mind. He decided eating was a good distraction, especially since he hadn't had any breakfast. He walked to the fireplace and set the flashlight, nose up, on the mantel. Then he stooped down to where he'd left his bag.

He spread open the bag's edges so that the glow from the flashlight would catch on the contents, and then sifted around until he found the one-liter bottle of soda he'd packed the night before he left.

"What's that?"

He looked up, unaware that Rachel had followed him back across the room. He held the cylindrical bottle up for her to see. "Complimentary drinks from the management." He reached for the can of potato chips he'd seen hiding beneath his thermal blanket and took those out too. "A feast fit for a king," he said, smiling.

He sat down on the floor and waited for Rachel to join him. He knew she would. Her curiosity over the things he was holding in his hands wouldn't let her do anything else.

He tried not to feel too confident when she settled down beside him. The last thing he wanted to do was scare her away again. "Your drink, madame," he said, and handed her the bottle of soda.

She stared at it, turned it around in the dim light, and then grimaced. "Dr . . . Pepper?"

"It's pop."

"Pop?"

"Soda pop." He reached out and twisted off the lid, and she frowned at the swish of escaping carbon dioxide. "Have a taste."

She looked at the bottle, cringed some more, and then handed it to him. "You taste it."

He accepted the bottle from her, set it to his bottom lip, and took a long swig. The burn was great, all the way down. "Ahhh," he said, and smacked his lips. "Now you."

Giving him a suspicious frown, still she accepted the bottle from him. "I don't drink alcohol."

"It's not alcohol."

She sniffed it. Then she tentatively touched her little pink tongue to the top edge and Scott thought his pounding heart was going to crack his chest. Finally, she set her mouth over the top, tipped the bottle until the soda had barely entered her mouth, and then quickly lowered it.

She blinked, licked her lips, and then looked at him in surprise. "It's soda water. But what flavor is . . ."— she peered at the bottle again—"Dr Pepper?"

"There's a question for the scientists," Scott replied. He held up the can of potato chips, anticipating how she might investigate them. "Hungry?"

With the curious look of a child, she carefully took the long red can from him. "Pringles . . . Original . . . Potato . . . Crisps," she read slowly. She took off the plastic lid and encountered the daunting "stay fresh" seal. She turned the can over and stared at the metal bottom, and then arched a brow at Scott. "There's food in here?"

Scott took another swig of soda, and then reached over, grabbed hold of the "stay fresh" tab, and drew back the paper from the opening. "Help yourself."

She stuck two fingers inside and then quickly pulled them back out. She rubbed her fingers together, and then touched them to her tongue. God, he wanted that tongue. Wanted it tangling with his own and then slipping into his mouth. She gave him a curious look, and he flashed her a quick smile, hoping she couldn't see the overpowering desire burning in his eyes.

He took another drink as she reached back into the can and pulled out a small stack of chips. She stared at them, tapped at them with her finger, and then turned and held one out to him. Again, he was to be her guinea pig.

He leaned forward and took the salty chip into his mouth, being sure to get just a tiny taste of her fingers in the bargain. He chewed loudly, and she laughed.

Finally she took a small bite of her own. "Mmmm," she said after a moment. "Salty."

Scott handed her the soda. "No backwashing," he warned, and leaned back over toward his duffle bag for something else he thought she might like. Or rather, something else he thought he might enjoy watching her eat. But Rachel's sudden cry of panic stopped him cold.

A fuzzy, black and white creature came scurrying across the floor toward them, and Rachel's heart leapt in her chest. "Don't move," Scott Ramsey told her.

She certainly didn't have to be told that twice.

"He smells our food," he said.

"And we're about to start smelling something even worse," she replied under her breath.

"Toss him a chip. Slowly."

Rachel threw the skunk the potato chip she'd been munching on, and the vile little rodent made a beeline for it and ate it in one ravenous bite.

"Now toss him another one a little closer to the door."

"But *I'm* a little closer to the door," she retorted in a harsh whisper.

"Just don't move any more than you have to."

Apparently the rule didn't apply to Scott because as Rachel continued to throw the potato crips, leading the animal toward the door, Scott slowly climbed to his feet and moved toward the pile of broken furniture in the corner. Finally, the skunk was only a few feet from the door—and Rachel.

Scott carefully stepped up behind it as it continued eating, and swung back the long piece of wood. Thinking he meant to kill the animal, Rachel squeezed her eyes shut and turned her head. But instead of a thud she heard a soft scraping sound, and turned to see the skunk go sailing out the front door. The animal hit the ground running, and hurried off into the woods.

"Well," Scott said, tossing his makeshift broom back into the scrap pile. "That didn't cause too much of a stink."

Rachel rolled her eyes and scratched where the dirty neckline of her dress was beginning to irritate her skin.

His eyes followed her movements. "I thought you were going to change your clothes."

And take them off with him there? After all the intent stares he'd been giving her in the past few minutes, Rachel wasn't so sure that was such a good idea. She didn't know if she could trust him, and she knew she couldn't trust herself—that had pretty well been proven to her the night before. No, she'd suffer through until her brothers arrived to prevent either of them from getting any wild ideas.

Scott Ramsey was bending over his black bag again, doing something that was making a faint crackling sound. Finally, he sat back down beside her, their thighs touching, their arms touching, and held out his fist, palm down. "Open your hand," he said to her.

Intrigued by what he might show her next, she did as he asked and held out her open hand. Small, brightly colored pebbles dribbled into her palm, and she nudged them around with her finger for a moment before giving him a questioning look. "What are these for?"

She watched, fascinated, as he picked one of them up and popped it into his mouth. Amazingly enough, he chewed up the pebble—and then reached for another.

Thinking this was the oddest thing she'd ever seen, Rachel took one between her thumb and forefinger and tested it with her front teeth. It broke in half, half of it falling into her mouth. She almost pushed it out with her tongue, but then she got a taste of something sweet and realized it was chocolate. They weren't pebbles at all, but tiny bits of colorful chocolate.

She took three more out of her hand, put them in her mouth, and looked up to find Scott smiling down at her. "I figured you for a sweet tooth," he said, dropping a gigantic, shiny brown bag full of chocolate pebbles into her lap.

Rachel felt like a child at Christmas. "Where on earth did you get all of these wonderful things?"

He looked away, shrugging. "Here and there."

He shifted, and his body rubbed against hers, causing her breath to catch. "I . . . I suppose you really *must* be well traveled."

He smirked. "You could say that."

"Then do you spy for other countries?" She'd heard of men like that; mercenaries, her brothers called them.

He let out a long, impatient sigh. Then he reached over and took her by the chin. "I'm going to say this to you one more time, Rachel Ann Warren. I am *not* a spy."

She stared into his shadowed eyes, and wondered why he continued to deny the obvious. Didn't he trust her?

"It's because I'm a woman, isn't it?" she blurted.

His hand dropped from her face. "What?"

"That's why you won't be honest with me about your mission."

"That has nothing to do with it."

"Ha! So, you *are* hiding something from me."

"Jesus. Yes, Rachel, you're right," he said dryly. "I *am* hiding something from you. The truth is, I'm a time-traveler from one hundred and forty years in the future."

She stared at him, not sure whether to be angry with him for not trusting her, or angry with herself for caring. She looked away. "Fine. I don't care what your silly mission is anyway." She put a few more of the chocolate pebbles into her mouth and folded her arms stubbornly across her chest. *Time-traveler,* she thought irritably as a slight chill shook through her.

"Come here," he said, wrapping his arm around her shoulders.

"What is it?" He was pulling her closer and she wasn't at all sure she should be letting him.

"It's cold and damp here in the deep, dark jungle, and I thought I'd do the gentlemanly thing and try to keep you warm."

She *was* a little chilled. And all he was doing was holding her close. So she tried relaxing against him, closing her eyes and listening to his even breathing, but the sound of her own pounding heart kept getting in the

way. And she wished he'd stop caressing her shoulder—
but then, she wished he'd never stop. . . .

"Will you be heading north after today?" she asked
after a few tense moments, hoping a little conversation
might distract them both.

"In a roundabout way."

"Then I'd like to extend an invitation for you to stay
at my family's home."

He paused. "And how would your family feel about
that?"

"My parents would enjoy meeting you. And I'm sure
they'd want to thank you for . . . for . . ."

"For saving you from the skunk?"

She smiled playfully. "Do you think the offer *stinks*?"
His chest rumbled with his gentle laughter.

"I'll think about it."

She tipped her head back against his arm and looked
up at him in all seriousness. "Promise?"

His expression instantly sobered. "Rachel . . . I'm
afraid it's not possible."

She'd been certain that he would accept her invitation, and was profoundly disappointed by his refusal.
"You have another mission after this one?"

"Yes."

"Then when you leave . . . I won't ever see you
again?" That same hot stare was coming back into his
eyes, and this time Rachel couldn't find the will to pull
away. She could no longer arm herself with the knowl-
edge that he was a *confederate* pirate. The truth was, he
was a compatriot, a man with her convictions and values.
And she realized in that moment that she was now completely vulnerable to his charm, his touch, and the heart-
stopping power of his incomparable kisses.

16

His kisses were like strong, sweet wine that flooded Rachel's senses and made her dizzy with desire.

Scott had taken her onto his lap, and she was being cradled in his arms as he sampled hungrily from her mouth. His hand was moving on a slow titillating journey from her waist to the rapid rise and fall of her breasts, and she caught her breath as he skimmed his palm slowly up one rounded slope.

Then his mouth left hers, dragging over her jaw and down the exposed curve of her throat. "I want you, Rachel," he whispered. "I want you so bad."

She knew, instinctively, what he meant, and there was no hesitation as she curled her arm behind his back and pressed against his warm hand. His fingers squeezed her, molding her to his palm, and a little moan pulled from the back of her throat.

He slipped her wedding gown from her shoulder, as he seemed on a mission to find new places to kiss her. His hand left her breast and she soon felt it on her ankle, then on her calf, then the back of her knee as his fingers slipped beneath the hem of her lace-edged drawers.

"These things cover too much of your sexy legs," he whispered, making her pulse race.

He kissed her neckline lower, and lower, moving the sleeve of her dress further and further down her arm, until she felt the warmth of his breath on her breast. She remembered the incredible sensation of him suckling her the night before through her nightgown, and instinctively arched toward him.

He circled her nipple with the smooth, hot glide of his tongue as his hand moved up her skirt to her stomach. He found the tie that held up her drawers, and she felt a tug, then the warmth of his hand on her bare skin as he nudged them down over her hips. It dawned on Rachel that he was undressing her, and one last vestige of apprehension made her stiffen in his arms.

"No, don't fight it," he whispered. "Don't fight me this time, Rachel."

His words alone had the power to entice her, and she once again relaxed into his arms. He'd reached beyond her hips and had hooked his fingers along the back waistband of her drawers. Now he began to slowly slip them off her. She didn't resist when he shifted her slightly, but she did let out a deep groan once he'd tossed her drawers aside and then slid his strong hand all the way up her bare leg to take a possessive grip on her bottom.

He dragged kisses up her throat toward her lips, and then had another thorough taste of her mouth. His tongue plunged and his teeth nibbled, and she thought she would lose her mind before he finally pulled back from her.

He stood with her cradled in his arms and carried her across the room to the cot. She clung to his neck, placing kisses on the hard line of his jaw as he fought to untie the string binding her bedroll. But it was an impossible task for one hand.

Finally he sat down on the edge of the wood and placed her straddling his thighs. He shoved her wedding dress up past her hips and placed his hand back on her naked bottom as he kissed the curve of her neck. His other hand began deftly unbuttoning the back of her gown.

The material parted, and Rachel felt the heat of his palm through the thin linen of her chemise. "No corset?" he said with a ragged whisper. "One less thing to strip off you. Lift your arms."

Rachel didn't hesitate, even though she knew that the gown was the last barrier between them, the last hope she had of resisting. But she didn't want to resist. She wanted to feel every touch, every taste, every kiss he had to offer, and then beg him for more.

He took hold of the hem of her dress and the edge of her chemise, and drew them both over her head at the same time in one smooth motion. The fabric caught on her breasts, grazing her sensitized nipples, and she closed her eyes while the veil of material skimmed up over her face. Then he went still, and there was only the sound of their quick, ragged breathing in the quiet dimness of the cabin.

Finally she opened her eyes and found him staring at her, running his eyes over every bare inch of her body. She remained motionless in the position he'd placed her over his thighs, until she felt the heat of his hands over her thighs, her hips, her bottom, her back, until they came to rest just below her breasts. That's when his eyes lifted to hers.

"You're so beautiful," he said in a soft, intent voice that left no doubt of his sincerity.

She smiled, shyly, and began working loose the buttons on the front of his shirt. He watched her in silence, unmoving, and she felt a moment of power when she pushed the garment from his broad, muscular shoulders. He lowered his arms just long enough for her to completely remove his shirt, and then returned his hands to their place beneath her breasts.

She was infatuated with the ridges and plateaus of his upper body; she had been since watching him bathe in the pond the day before. He was chiseled like an ancient marble statue. She brushed her fingers over his skin, using both hands to map the hard structure of his chest and shoulders.

"The sight of you makes . . . makes me weak," she admitted breathlessly.

"I know the feeling," he replied.

He pulled her closer, flattening her breasts against his chest. And she kissed him this time, moving her mouth in a long, sweet slide over his. She placed warm, lingering kisses along his jaw, and then enjoyed the salty taste of his neck. He groaned, took hold of her bottom, and pressed her toward him. And that's when she felt the hard, long ridge of his desire bulge up against the apex of her thighs. As it had been the night before with the pressure of his leg, Rachel instinctively moved against him and felt the sharp, sweet pressure begin to build within her again.

Scott let out an agonizing groan, and, using both hands, yanked open the buttons on the opening of his pants. Then he took hold of her bottom and moved her even closer, pressed her up against the silken heat of his desire.

"Oh God, Rachel," he gritted out, biting at her chin. He slipped his hands beneath her thighs and lifted her over the broad, hot tip of him.

Rachel waited for more, waited for him to lower her down and fulfill this aching need raging inside of her, but he didn't. His tight grip on her thighs remained, increased in fact, but he didn't move her another inch. She pulled back, thinking something was wrong, and almost gasped at the fierce passion burning in his eyes.

"The decision is still yours," he said to her, although she could see him fighting for restraint.

As far as Rachel was concerned, there was no decision left to be made. She relaxed the tightened muscles in her thighs and slowly sank down over him.

He pulled in a sharp breath, and she closed her eyes as his steely flesh filled her. There was a brief, quickly forgotten stab of pain, and then nothing but the tight delicious pressure of him embedded deeply inside her.

She dropped her forehead to his shoulder and struggled to control her breathing.

His lips, soft and warm, moved over her shoulder as he made slow, subtle movements with his hips that sent bursts of pleasure shooting through her. He placed his hands on her waist and lifted her slightly. The friction made her groan.

He lifted her again, and this time she arched back, losing herself in the moment, and he began to feast on one of her tight, rigid nipples. Alone these two sensations were incredible, but together they were overwhelming.

Those same tightening sensations from the night before came back to Rachel, urging her to move in a sensual rhythm all her own. Finally her world burst open in a dazzling explosion of stars, and she felt herself squeezing at the man inside of her, as if her body were urging his to join her. He let out a low growl. His grip on her legs tightened and his hips lifted from the cot beneath him, embedding him even deeper than before. He pulsed inside of her, and cried out her name. And it was in that magical moment that Rachel Ann Warren realized she'd fallen deeply and unequivocally in love.

Scott helped Rachel slip into his discarded shirt, and then he buttoned it up the front over her breasts. It draped her small frame, covering her from her shoulders to the tops of her knees, but the damn thing had never looked better.

He'd untied the bedroll her brothers had left, and spread it out over the wooden cot. And now he helped her slip in between the blankets. She looked as exhausted as he felt, and he climbed in beside her and pulled her to him. Almost immediately she fell into a pattern of deep, even breathing, and he knew the instant she fell asleep in his arms.

In the stillness of the cabin, he buried his face in her hair and considered the ramifications of what they'd just done. He'd made love to women before, but never like this, never with his whole heart and soul. How in the world was he ever going to bring himself to leave her?

Rachel stirred against him and he kissed the top of her head. She was a strong, intelligent woman, and he knew she'd go on to live a full and happy life without him. But that "without him" part sure hurt like hell.

17

Scott woke to the feel of something cold being pressed between his eyes. He opened them, and found himself staring up into the long twin barrels of a shotgun. There were two men standing over him, one dark-haired and one light-haired, and both were glaring at him with murder in their eyes.

"Who the hell are you?" the light-haired man demanded. Rachel stirred against Scott's chest, and he pulled her closer. He'd die before he'd let either one of these men touch her.

"Who cares who he is," the darker man holding the shotgun said. "After what he's done to our sister, he's wolf meat."

Their *sister*? *Uh-oh,* Scott gave Rachel a gentle shake. She moaned, and then slid up his body to bury her face in his neck. He closed his eyes, trying to resist the desire he could feel stirring within him even now. "Rachel?" he whispered in her ear.

"Hmmm?"

"Wake up."

"*You* wake me up," she replied with a sexy, sleepy giggle.

The man standing with the shotgun clenched his teeth and Scott gave him a hesitant smile. "Rachel, sweetheart?" Scott said carefully. "If you don't open your little eyes and tell these two pit bulls to 'heel,' I'll be getting buckshot in my face."

Rachel pulled away from him, frowning. Then she followed the direction of his stare and her eyes widened on her brothers. "Jeremy! Zach!" She attempted to sit up, but the cot was too small for her to manage it. "It isn't dark!" she said accusingly.

"We decided not to wait till dark," the blond man replied. "We were *worried* about you."

"What the devil is going on here, Rachel Ann?" the dark brother demanded.

"Put that shotgun down, Jeremy." Rachel shoved at the twin barrels. She had to climb over the top of Scott, but managed to slip off the cot without too much trouble, and then she adjusted the hem of his shirt against her knees.

"Did he *force* you?" Jeremy demanded. "Because if he did—"

"He didn't force me," Rachel replied adamantly. "Captain Ramsey and I—"

"The *pirate?*" Jeremy demanded, and brought the shotgun back up to Scott's face.

"Oh, stop it, Jeremy. I *know* he isn't a pirate."

"He isn't?" blond Zach replied.

"I am well aware that he is a spy, just like me."

Both of Rachel's brothers narrowed pale green glares on Scott, and he groaned and fell back on the cot. "Is *that* what he told you?" Jeremy demanded.

"Of course not. He would never admit his mission to me or anybody else."

Jeremy was giving his sister a dumbfounded look. "Have you lost your mind?"

Rachel scowled and cast Scott a hesitant glance. "I've decided to forgive you two for sending him to keep track of me."

"Rachel Ann, we've never seen this man before in our lives," Zach said soberly.

Scott swung his legs over the edge of the cot, hating the look of suspicion that was growing in Rachel's eyes. "Rachel—"

"Of course you have!" she interrupted. "Don't lie to me, Zach!"

"Rachel Ann, honey, I'm not lyin' to you. I don't know who the hell this man is."

With a cry of shock and anguish, Rachel turned and stared disbelievingly at Scott. "Rachel," he began again. "I kept telling you, and telling you—"

"You lied to me *again*!" she cried.

"I have *never* lied to you, damn it!" Scott said, lurching to his feet. "You just keep *jumping* to all the wrong conclusions!"

"This shotgun's gonna be jumping down your throat," Jeremy said to him, "if you don't sit yourself back down there, mister."

"Who are you—*really*!" she demanded.

"I'm Captain Scott Ramsey," he replied impatiently. "Have you noticed how that answer never changes?"

"Captain of what?" Jeremy asked, his eyes narrowed suspiciously.

"I can't tell you that."

"Hell," the man swore. "He's probably working for Uncle Thomas. There's every chance our uncle grew suspicious of Rachel and sent this fellow to capture us all."

"That's not true," Scott said. "I'm not a Confederate."

"Then you're with the Union?" Zach asked.

Scott sighed. "Let's just say I'm *for* the Union."

"Prove it," Jeremy stated.

"And how am I supposed to do that?" Scott was keeping his eyes on Rachel as she backed away to the other side of the room. "I don't exactly have the stars and stripes tattooed across my chest."

"Where are you from?" Jeremy demanded.

"Washington."

"The capital?" Zach asked.

No, the state. "Look what does it matter where I'm from. I'm all *for* Lincoln and the Emancipation Proclamation."

"The what?" Zach's eyes were intense as he exchanged a glance with his brother. And then they both gave Scott a hard stare.

Scott figured he'd really screwed up, and let go with a nervous laugh. "Hasn't that thing been signed yet?"

"I oughta blow your head off for what you've done to my sister, Captain," Jeremy said coldly. "And it doesn't matter to me if you're Union."

"Only the highest officials in Washington know about the Proclamation," Zach said. He was walking across the room toward Rachel, who was still looking too stricken for Scott's peace of mind. "Jeremy and I would have never heard of it if General Garfield hadn't mentioned it."

"Then he's telling the truth?" Rachel whispered. "He is on our side?"

"He seems to be."

Scott sighed in relief. "Now could you get this pellet blower out of my face?"

"No sudden moves, Captain," Jeremy warned, lowering the shotgun. "You may be Union, but that doesn't mean I have to like you."

"Jeremy?" Zach called.

"Yeah?"

"Have a look at this."

Scott looked over to see that Zach was holding up the wedding dress. One more reminder that this stranger had seduced their sister.

"So?" Jeremy stated.

Zach sighed, rolling his eyes in a perfect imitation of Rachel, and held the dress out a little further. "Jeremy," he said. "This is a wedding dress."

Rachel snatched the gown from her brother's hands. "It's a ruined wedding dress is what it is."

"When the hell did this happen, Rachel Ann?" Jeremy demanded.

"This morning," Rachel replied. "I managed—"

"And were you planning on telling us before or after I put a barrel of buckshot in your new husband, here?"

"My hus—"

"This whole picture makes a world of difference if you're married, Rachel Ann," Zach cut in, beginning to smile.

"And I've been standing here with my finger on this trigger trying not to picture Mother's face while I explain all this to her. Thank God I was spared from that."

Scott stared at the two brothers in complete exasperation. Good Christ, did this entire family do nothing but jump to conclusions? He looked over at Rachel, waiting for her to explain that they weren't married. The very last thing he expected her to do was lie.

"I . . . I wanted to tell you . . . but you haven't exactly given either one of us a chance to explain anything," she replied.

"Are you happy about this?" Zach asked.

Rachel walked toward Scott, her eyes glittering with

a warning for him not to contradict her. "Yes," she replied, taking hold of his arm. "Deliriously."

Zach stepped forward. "My apologies, Ramsey," he said, and Scott warily shook his hand.

"Where's the ring?" Jeremy replied.

"We had no time for silly things like that this morning, Jeremy," Rachel said quickly. "The minister was unhappy about being woken up so early, and Scott and I needed to hurry before Uncle Thomas woke to find me and his money gone. Right . . . honey?" she said to Scott, adding a smile for punctuation.

Scott didn't know what the hell she was doing, or why. But at this point he was willing to do almost anything to patch up this mess—for his sake and for hers. "You know how impetuous young love can be," he said, smiling back at her.

"You couldn't wait until we got home?" Jeremy asked. "Until Mother and Father had met him?"

"We couldn't wait a *moment* longer, Jeremy," Rachel insisted.

"That's pretty apparent," Zach remarked.

Rachel turned a charming shade of red, and Scott gave her hand a squeeze. "Like she said, we didn't expect you two until after dark. And what else would newlyweds do to occupy their time?"

That last remark got him a sharp poke in the ribs from Rachel, and Zach broke into a grin. "I think I'm gonna like this fellow, Jeremy."

Jeremy's scowl said that he didn't quite agree. But he stuck his hand out to Scott anyway. "Welcome to the family, Ramsey," he said. "And if you hurt my sister, I'll break your neck."

*   *   *

All right, so maybe they weren't really married. Rachel had only let her brothers believe that in order to save herself from the embarrassment of having to face her mother with the news of her shameful conduct. But after a few hours of pretending to be Scott Ramsey's wife, she was starting to get used to the idea, and she had to admit that she liked the way it felt: being able to sit on the floor beside him and hold his hand; feeling his heavy arm around her even when her brothers were just a few feet away.

So he wasn't a spy. He had tried to tell her that fact several times, so she supposed she couldn't hold him responsible for the mix-up. Still there was a shroud of mystery surrounding him. He was obviously involved in something very top-secret for the government, and although she was dying to know what it was, she'd decided not to press him about it just yet.

She was lying on her stomach on the cot, with her chin propped on her fist as she listened to her brothers and "husband" plot their escape from Georgia the following morning. Zach had immediately accepted Scott as his new brother-in-law, but stubborn Jeremy was still holding back. He had always been just a little too protective of her.

"What are you grinning about over there?" Zach called to her. The three of them were sitting on the floor in the glow of the flashlight, munching on those salty potato crips from Scott's bag.

"Can't I just be happy, Zach Warren?" she sassed back.

"Let this be a lesson to you, Ramsey," Zach said. "Our sister is never 'just happy.' She's always got designs."

Scott smiled over at Rachel and her heart pounded in her chest. "I'll keep that in mind," he replied.

"You can both do all the designing you like," Jeremy stated, "as soon as we figure a safe way out of enemy territory."

"I think a straight shot north is indisputably the best course to take," Zach said. "Straight and steady."

Jeremy nodded. "We could take the old Gunnison Road up through Reevestown, cut across to Devonsburg, and on into Milledgeville."

"From there," Zach said, chewing the potato crips loud enough that Rachel could hear them all the way across the room, "we catch a train to Knoxville."

"Then we ride across the border into Kentucky," Jeremy added.

"Well you two certainly have it all figured out," Rachel remarked. "But there's one problem with your little plan."

"What's that?" Zach asked.

"The dogs."

"Uncle Thomas wouldn't do that, Rachel Ann," Jeremy replied. "We're not exactly a band of runaway slaves."

"Jeremy Warren," Rachel said, sitting up. "We just stole ten thousand of the man's hard-earned dollars. I think he'll employ whatever means possible to find us."

"She's got a point," Scott said. "I just spent three days with him, and in my opinion, if he's got blood-hounds he'll use them."

Jeremy studied Scott carefully. "Then we'll have a contingency plan."

Rachel slipped off the edge of the cot, adjusting Scott's shirt around her legs, and walked toward where they were sitting on the floor. "We should head straight up the Altamaha and into the Oconee," she said.

"You want to *swim* into Milledgeville?" Zach said, smiling.

"We ride along the banks, dipping into the water when it's shallow enough. Our scent will be washed away, and the dogs will never be able to track us."

Her brothers both blinked at her in surprise. "Sounds like a solid plan to me," Scott said.

"Yeah," Zach said, shrugging. "Sounds good, Rachel Ann."

But Jeremy still wasn't convinced. "A straight shot would be faster."

"It won't matter how fast we're going if we're captured," Rachel replied.

Jeremy stared at her, his expression stony. "You're getting a little too clever for your own good, Rachel Ann."

"And that is the nicest compliment you have ever paid me, Jeremy David Warren. Keep that up and I'll start to think you actually appreciate me."

"Go back to bed, you little scamp," Jeremy grumbled, beginning to smile. "And if I forget to tell you later, you did good work. Really good work."

Rachel stepped forward and gave him a kiss on the cheek. "Don't forget me," Zach called, pointing to his own cheek.

Rachel laughed and moved around the circle to give her other brother a buss as well. And then she came to Scott. He was staring up at her, his eyes burning with an inner light, and Zach nudged her on the back of the leg. "Don't be shy, Rachel Ann. Give your husband a kiss."

She swallowed, and set her hands on Scott's shoulders. "Good night," she whispered.

He lifted his face up to her, and she closed her eyes and pressed her mouth to his. Her stomach flipped when she felt the quick stab of his tongue against her lips. "Good night," he said back.

"Go keep the bed warm for him," Jeremy grumbled. "We won't keep him much longer."

Rachel felt another blush coming on. She hurried across the dimly lit floor and practically dove beneath the blankets of her bedroll. Scott was going to sleep with her? With her brothers sacked right there with them? But then what had she expected? For all intents and purposes . . . the two of them were married.

18

Before the invention of television, man apparently amused himself very easily. Scott realized this while watching Zach Warren try to balance an M&M's candy on the end of his nose and then drop it into his mouth. There was a small, multicolored stain beginning to show just above his left nostril.

"So you were sent here to observe?" Jeremy was asking.

"Right," Scott replied. He laughed as Zach tried and failed once again with the M&M's.

"Not to *act*?"

"No. Rachel sort of pulled me into the situation by mistaking me for your uncle's pirate captain."

"But I still don't understand who sent you. And why."

Scott had been answering Jeremy's questions to the best of his ability, but there were just some things Jeremy was going to have to let slide. "I can't tell you that."

"But you *are* a member of the United States military?"

"Yes."

Jeremy sighed, and then shrugged. "I suppose that's all that really matters—damnation, would you listen to that wind?" he added frowning at the open doorway. "Sounds like a hurricane picking up out there."

Scott blinked, and then his attention was instantly drawn to the door. "Yeah—listen," he said, "I'm gonna go answer the call of nature. I'll be right back."

He stood from the floor, and stole a glance at Rachel. She was still sleeping soundly. Dreading what he was going to find, he walked toward the front door.

The time-portal was fixed. The thing was as big as life, and not so aggressive as before. It was whooshing and whirling just beyond the walls of the cabin, making Zach and Jeremy's three horses toss their heads nervously.

Scott watched it for a while, letting reality sink in. It was over. It was time to go home where he belonged.

But it's too soon, he told himself. How could he leave without being sure that Rachel made it across the Mason-Dixon line? No, he refused to leave until he was sure she'd gotten away safely. The future was just going to have to wait one more night.

He picked up a branch from the ground and tossed it through the portal. The door immediately sucked closed, and Scott found himself standing in the dark forest with a billion crickets chirping in the warm night air. He felt an intense surge of relief.

When he stepped back into the cabin, Jeremy and Zach stood and announced their intention to bed down for the night. They planned to sleep outside and give the two "newlyweds" the cabin to themselves.

"See you in the morning, Ramsey," Zach called.

"At first light," Jeremy added.

They left the cabin and Scott crossed the room for

the flashlight on the mantel. The glow was quite a bit dimmer than it had been earlier that day. He turned it off and put it into his duffle bag, then he walked through the darkness toward the cot where Rachel was still sleeping all snuggled and warm.

He slipped out of his jeans, leaving his underwear on as he eased beside her beneath the blankets. The cot was narrow, giving him a good excuse to press up against her back. She murmured in her sleep as he bent his legs into the curve of hers. He pressed his face into the back of her hair, and the subtle smell of her alone was enough to get his heart going. She shifted back against him, and immediately he felt his passion rise.

She was still wearing his shirt. He took hold of the bottom edge and lifted it just enough to slip his hand beneath. Her skin felt as soft as rose petals as he ran his fingers up the outer edge of her thigh and curled them around her hip bone. She shifted again, bringing her leg back and hooking her knee behind his.

The sensitive tip of him felt the heat between her legs, and he pressed his face into her hair, barely withholding a groan. No woman had ever had this kind of power over him before.

Her hips wiggled, and Scott sucked in a breath. Finally, he nudged open the fly on his boxers, releasing himself to press fully against her. He slipped his hand up the outside of the shirt to begin undoing the buttons. Three was all it took before he was able to caress one of her breasts. Her nipple hardened instantly against his palm, and he gently worked the sensitive nub.

Rachel groaned softly, and pressed her head back into the crook of his neck. He bent forward and tasted the soft, sweet skin of her shoulder. "Do you mind if I play husband?" he whispered.

"Mmmm," she replied sleepily, and pressed back against him in a way that made his blood surge.

It took him all of two seconds to get the rest of her shirt unbuttoned, and then he was tangling his fingers in the crisp curls at the base of her flat stomach. He heard her breath catch.

He gently sank his teeth into her shoulder as he slipped his fingers down the groove of her sex. She was ready for him, and instinctively lifted her leg, giving him greater access. With one smooth thrust he was inside her.

She gasped in surprise and moaned, and he wrapped his arm around her stomach trying desperately to remain in control of himself. "Shhhh," he whispered, nibbling on her ear. "Arch your back. Ummm, that's right."

Her hand crept back and took hold of his thigh. He smiled against her neck as she pulled him closer, urging him onward. He rotated his hips, just a little, and her grip on his leg tightened. He pressed into her, and then pulled back, and she arched her little bottom toward him, wanting more.

Scott took a firm hold around her waist with his arm, and started up a steady rhythm that soon had them both breathing hard. She was close, so close, he could feel it in the small trembles of her body. Finally her entire body tightened. And with one more steady thrust he made her tumble over the top. She dug her nails into his thigh as her body squeezed at him, again and again. She said his name on the raspy wings of a sigh, and that's when he let himself go. He pulsed inside her, driving his hips against her, until they both went still in pleasant exhaustion.

She shifted and turned toward him. It was too dark in the cabin to see her face, so Scott kissed her, loving the taste of her, the feel of her against him.

"I'm sorry that I dragged you into an unwanted marriage," she whispered playfully a few moments later.

"There's nobody I'd rather have drag me."

"Then maybe I can get you to reconsider that visit to my family's home?" she asked, a faint tremor in her voice.

Scott closed his eyes, wishing he didn't have to hurt her this way. "Rachel . . . I told you, it's not possible for me to do that."

"You're already married, aren't you."

"No," he replied, running his hand through her hair and setting his forehead against hers. "There's no one else but you."

"Then why—"

"My job is going to take me away." Christ, he wished he could see into her eyes so he could gauge her emotions. "Once you reach the Mason-Dixon line, I'll be leaving."

"Where will you go?"

"I can't tell you—God, I wish I could, Rachel. I wish so many damn things."

"I understand."

But her tone said she didn't. He'd never felt this strongly for anyone before in his life, and he couldn't even reassure her. "If I could stay with you I would. I *swear* it."

He brushed his thumb over her satiny cheek and felt the dampness of tears. "Then there's no hope?" she whispered.

He wrapped his arms around her and pulled her close, kissing away her tears. " There's only right now."

*   *   *

Dawn came too early for Rachel. The sun was just a crimson glow in the eastern sky when Jeremy came into the cabin and told her and Scott to "roll out of bed." Rachel had been awake for hours, not wanting to waste a precious second of the time she had left with the man she loved.

Scott stirred, and glanced down to where her head was lying against his shoulder. He smiled at her, and the gesture brought tears burning at the back of her eyes. But despite the ache in her heart, she refused to make him feel guilty about choosing his work over her. The last thing in the world she needed was for the man she loved to hate her for convincing him to give up his way of life. She would take the memories he'd given her, and pray that someday he'd grow tired of wandering and return to her.

He rolled from the cot and helped her to her feet. "I don't get the impression that your brother is a very patient man," he said, smoothing the hair back out of her face. "You should probably hurry and change. I'll wait for you outside."

"I'll wait for you forever," she said softly to him.

He closed his eyes as if her words had caused him a great deal of pain, and then he bent and gave her a soft, lingering kiss. "Don't cheat yourself, Rachel. I expect you to go on with your life."

"I will love you till the end of time, Scott Ramsey," she said, unable to stop tears from welling in her eyes.

He pulled her to him in a crushing embrace and buried his lips against her neck. She could feel his emotions surging through him, and then he pulled away. He gathered up his pants and boots, and walked from the cabin.

Rachel gave in to her tears for a moment, needing the release to keep from embarrassing herself in front of her brothers, and then, with shaking fingers, she unbuttoned the shirt Scott had loaned her. His scent still clung to the sleek, soft cotton, and she pressed it to her face before laying it down on the cot.

She opened the satchel her brothers had left for her and took out a blue skirt and simple white shirt. She dressed quickly, but was still tying her shoes when Jeremy called for her to hurry. "We're wastin' light, Rachel Ann," he called. She gathered up her things and hurried outside.

Zach took her bedroll from her and wound it up tight, while Scott went back into the cabin to gather his things. When he returned a few minutes later, his black bag in his hand, Rachel handed him his shirt. "I thought about keeping it," she said softly. "But then I realized that you don't have anything else to wear."

He smiled gently at her, took the shirt, and slipped it on.

"Come on, you two," Zach called. He and Jeremy were already mounted up. "You can whisper sweet things to each other in the saddle."

Not expecting their sister to bring anyone else along on her grand escape, Jeremy and Zach had brought only three horses. So Scott and Rachel had to ride double. She sat in front of him in the saddle, holding his black bag, as he guided their horse along behind her two brothers.

They were heading for the Altamaha River. It would take them straight to the Oconee which would lead them due north. Barring any mishaps, they'd reach Milledgeville and be on a train for the northern Tennessee border before the end of the next day. After that it was just a matter of making a run for Kentucky. She'd be home within a week, but somehow knowing that didn't console Rachel as the horse beneath her plodded on, bringing her closer and closer to the moment when she and Scott would have to say good-bye.

*   *   *

They'd been riding for almost an hour, and during that time Rachel had been very quiet. Too quiet, as far as Scott was concerned.

Finally, he gave her a little squeeze. "Okay, Miss Ominous Silence, what are you thinking about?"

"You," she replied.

"A good me? Or a bad me?"

Her faint laugh acted like a soothing balm on his worries. "There's no such thing as a bad you, Scott Ramsey. . . . Maybe a *naughty* you."

"I like bein' naughty," he said and bent down to bite at her ear.

"Don't start getting so frisky you fall off that horse," Zach called to them.

"We're holding on," Rachel called back.

"Yeah, but I'd like you to hold on to the *horse*." Scott laughed along with Zach and Jeremy, while Rachel grumbled something about Zach's crude sense of humor. Then they all settled into silence as they plodded down the trail.

"Tell me about the places you've traveled," Rachel asked a few minutes later.

"What do you want to know?"

"Are there many more wonderful things like what you've shown me?"

"A few."

"Tell me about them," she said eagerly.

Christ, where should he start? "Well—"

"Stop!" Jeremy suddenly called from up ahead of them. "Anybody else hear that?"

They all held still and listened.

Zach shifted in his saddle, and looked in the direction they'd come. "It sounds like—"

"Dogs!" Rachel exclaimed, straightening. "They've brought out the dogs!"

"Let's ride!" Jeremy shouted.

Both Jeremy and Zach applied their heels to their horses and took off down the trail in a powerful burst of speed. Scott, holding Rachel on board with one hand and maneuvering his horse with the other, stayed right on their heels. They could all hear the clamor of the dogs, even over the pounding of their horses' hooves, and it wasn't long before they realized they weren't going to be able to outrun them.

They came to a fork in the trail and Jeremy was the first to pull up short. "We've got to split up!"

"No!" Rachel shouted.

"Scott, take her to the left, toward the river. Zach and I will follow the road to the right and try to lead them off your trail."

Scott knew how dangerous that proposal was, and he and Jeremy exchanged a meaningful glance. "I'll keep her safe," Scott promised.

Jeremy gave him a curt nod. "We'll meet you in Milledgeville."

"Milledgeville," Scott repeated, and applied his heels to his horse.

"No!" Rachel cried out. It broke Scott's heart to ignore her pleas, but all any of them wanted right now was to get her to safety.

She was in a precarious position on the front of the saddle, and Scott had to divide his efforts between holding on to her and holding on for dear life. They rounded a curve at a breakneck speed and he saw the river sparkling just down the hill. The sound of the dogs hadn't lessened any, and he wondered if Jeremy's dangerous ploy had even worked.

He urged the horse off the trail and went charging down the hill toward the water. They crashed through bushes, and trampled through plants, but didn't slow until they'd reached the banks of the Altamaha River.

Suddenly, Scott pulled his horse to a stop. Standing there, armed and waiting for them, were the backers of the Glennville fleet.

"Rachel, my dear," Thomas Clayborn said coolly. "You and your friend seem to be chargin' off in quite a hurry."

"Get off the horse," Harold Trolley demanded, leveling his rifle at them.

Scott figured his options were pretty clear. He could either do as they said, or get himself and Rachel killed by trying to get away. He clenched his jaw and swung down from the horse. Then he reached up and helped Rachel to the ground.

All four men were lined up in front of them. Thomas Clayborn. Harold Trolley. Charles Bodain. And of course Beauregard, looking red in the face, as usual.

"Where is it?" Thomas Clayborn demanded.

"Where's what?" Scott replied.

"The money, you mud-swilling Yankee!" Beauregard shouted.

Charles Bodain cocked the hammer on his rifle. "You either give it to us now, mister, or we'll shoot you where you stand."

"He doesn't have it," Rachel spoke up.

"Then who does?" Clayborn demanded, eyeing Scott's black bag in her hands.

"Nobody does," she replied. "I burned it."

Scott gave her a startled look. "You burned it?"

"You—you *burned* it!" Harold Trolley bellowed. "My God, Thomas, she's ruined us! Your niece has destroyed what little hope we had!"

Thomas Clayborn's face and neck turned a bright beet red. "I should have known better than to think common white trash could ever become truly Southern—"

"I never *wanted* to become Southern, you overfed rebel!" Rachel shouted back.

"She's one of them!" Beauregard stated angrily. "She's been one of them all along!"

Thomas Clayborn's eyes narrowed. "Then she will die like one of them," he said darkly. "Gentlemen. We have two Yankee spies here. Prepare your aims."

Scott shoved Rachel behind him as all four men cocked and leveled their rifles. "It wasn't her!" he insisted. "*I've* been the spy all along, and I *forced* her to help me!"

"Ready?" Thomas Clayborn said.

"*You can't do this!*" Scott cried as Rachel's fingers dug into his back.

"Aim."

Like a doorway to heaven, the time-portal whirled open just to Scott's left. The four men across from him, their rifles aimed and ready, hesitated. And in that moment Scott saw only one way of saving his life and that of the woman he loved.

Turning, he lifted Rachel up into his arms, and jumped into the safety of the future.

19

✧

Preparing to die, Rachel squeezed her eyes shut and pressed up against Scott's back as she waited for a bullet to tear through her body. Scott turned and swept her up into his arms, valiantly trying to protect her. Her heart swelled with love for him. If only they could have had more time together.

But the painful burn of rending flesh never came. Instead there was a bright, blinding flash of light, and then complete nothingness.

After a few moments the darkness dissipated, and an intense cold set in. Rachel felt as if she were floating on a soft cloud, and then realized that she was still in Scott's strong arms. She curled more tightly against him as the frigid cold penetrated her clothes and chilled her to the bone. Then the noise broke through her dazed senses, noise so loud and steady it made her ears ring. It was deafening, as if ten thousand trains were moving past her all at once.

Scott bent over her, pressing his face down into the

side of her neck. And then, as quickly as it had all begun, it stopped—the cold, the noise. Nothing was left but a brilliant white light.

Scott straightened. "Are you all right?" he asked frantically.

Rachel cracked open one eyelid. The first thing she saw was the blue of his shirt, but then she slowly lifted her head, and squinted into the light. They were in some sort of smooth-walled tunnel. "Yes. Yes, I'm all right," she replied. "This certainly isn't what I imagined heaven to be like."

"We're not in heaven," Scott replied, setting her on her feet.

"Well, we're certainly not standing on the riverbank anymore."

In that moment a large section of the wall behind them slowly opened like the mouth of a giant monster. Frightened more than she cared to admit, Rachel dropped Scott's bag and moved toward him, taking a tight grip on the front of his shirt. "We're not dead," he said, putting his arm around her shoulders.

A large, dark-haired man dressed in some type of dark blue uniform stepped into the open doorway and stared at both of them. "If this isn't heaven, then where are we?" she asked tremulously.

"We're sort of . . . at my house."

She gave him a bewildered scowl, and then turned to look again at the man who was now coming down three metal steps toward them. "Captain," the man said, wearing a crooked smile. "I was startin' to think you might be history."

Scott shook the man's outstretched hand. "Frankly, Colonel, so was I."

"I can imagine you must have been gettin' a little nervous," the man replied. "It took longer than we expected to correct the problem. Those damn adjustments we made to strengthen the portal took up too much energy and shrunk the damn thing." The man turned his attention to Rachel, his smile faltering a bit. "Appears you've brought back a souvenir."

"Colonel Tayback, this is Rachel Ann Warren," Scott replied. "Rachel suddenly felt the need to get away for a little while."

"Uh-huh," Colonel Tayback said. "Nice to meet you, Miss Warren." He and Scott exchanged a look.

"I know," Scott said. "But we were both in a dangerous situation when the portal popped open, and if I'd left her there she would have been killed."

A tall, thin man with short blond hair and spectacles appeared in the doorway beyond Colonel Tayback. He took one look at Rachel and went as white as his long coat. "Shuckson!" he shouted over his shoulder. "Set up the examination room!"

"Well," the colonel said, his smile returning. "Let's get on outa this tin can before we all freeze to death."

Rachel's teeth were chattering, but she didn't think it was because of the cold. If she hadn't died and gone to heaven, then where in the world was she? And how in the world had she gotten there?

She took one step toward the door and the whole room suddenly began to spin around her. Her knees buckled, and if it hadn't been for Scott's strong arm around her shoulders she would have dropped to the floor.

He paused for a moment to steady her. "Are you all right?" he asked.

She nodded.

"There's always a little dizziness for a few minutes afterward," he said, obviously trying to reassure her.

After what? she wanted scream.

He helped her up the three metal stairs, and out of the "tin can." Then they stepped into a room where three men dressed in long, white coats were waiting for them. The men converged around her, asking questions faster than she could possibly understand them. But Rachel was so enamored with all the sights and sounds around her that she wasn't listening anyway.

There were lights everywhere, on everything it seemed, flashing or glowing. And again there was noise, nothing deafening this time, but still a steady, low hum coming from every direction. The furniture appeared to be made up entirely of metal. Rachel stared at one particularly odd chair that had wheels on the bottom of it.

"Bring her into the examination room," the tall blond man was saying. He came at her, pointing a metal stick with a bright light on the end of it, and she flinched back from him.

"It's okay, Rachel," Scott said to her. "He only wants to examine you to be sure you came through all right."

A large metal box resting on the table beside her beeped, startling her. "Came through *what* all right?" she finally demanded. "Where am I!"

The man with the stick light came toward her again and Scott held out his arm to block his pursuit. "Give her a minute, Girney."

"Captain," the man said, "this woman has just traveled one hundred and thirty-nine years into a future that doesn't exist for her yet. She *needs* to be examined."

Rachel stared at Scott, not sure how to take what she'd just heard. "I've *what?*"

"I did it to save your life," Scott explained. "If I hadn't taken you through the portal you would have been shot."

"What portal? *Where are we?*" she demanded, beginning to feel a little frantic.

"This is where I live, Rachel."

"You said you lived in Washington!"

"This is Washington. This is the *state* of Washington."

"There is no state of Washington," she replied, her voice trembling.

"There is in the year 2001."

Rachel stumbled backward and collided with a small table holding an object with more lights and paper coming out of the top. It beeped, and then made a horrible grinding noise, and she backed away from it too. "Why are you lying to me!" she cried.

"I'm not lying, Rachel." She was shaking her head, still backing away, wishing there were someplace she could hide. "I know it's hard for you to believe," he continued, slowly pursuing her. "But think about it for a minute. I showed up out of nowhere, dressed in strange clothing, using words you didn't understand. I have strange toys, and strange food—"

"I don't believe you!" she shouted.

"Look around you, damn it!" He began picking up objects from the metal table beside him. "This is a telephone! This is a digital clock! This is a pencil—a basic writing tool. Have you ever seen anything like this before, Rachel?"

Hot tears sprang to her eyes, practically blinding her as she reached out and reluctantly took the thin yellow stick from his fingers. It had a metal band at one end and something soft and brown at the top. She'd never seen anything like it before in her life.

"Lead runs through the center of the wood so that when the tip wears down you can use a sharp blade and whittle it back again."

"How can you expect me to believe—"

"You'd rather believe that you've died and gone to some twisted sort of heaven?" he replied. "Rachel"—he came forward and she let him take her into his arms, his strong secure arms—"there's nothing for you to be afraid of here. I know it's all very strange, but everything is going to be all right."

He kissed the top of her head, and she sank into his embrace. "How is this possible?" she whispered, her heart still pounding.

"It just is," he whispered back. "Now you have to let these people examine you. We have to make sure that you're all right."

Rachel looked past his shoulder at the four people, including the colonel, who were staring at her expectantly. "They aren't going to hurt me, are they?"

He smiled at her. "I'll break their necks if they hurt you."

Smiling at his repeat of Jeremy's threat just the night before, Rachel nodded.

"You've got five minutes, Girney," Scott said.

Rachel allowed Scott to lead her across the floor toward a door with a glass window in it, and a long, horizontal window in the wall beside it. She could see white shelves in the room beyond the large window, along with a long white table.

As she stepped through the doorway behind Scott, something on the wall beside her began to chirp like a little bird. Colonel Tayback stepped forward and pulled half of the object off the wall, and then Rachel stared in bewilderment as he held that half to his ear and began talking to it.

She gave Scott a confused look, but he only smiled at her and led her further into the room. The three people in white coats followed behind them, and Rachel was instructed to lie down on the long, leathery-looking table.

"Everything's going to be all right," Scott told her once again as he took her around the waist and lifted her up onto the table. She lay back, but kept a tight grip on his hand. She was trying to be brave, but everything around her was just too strange.

"Captain," the colonel said. "Can I speak to you outside?"

Scott gave Rachel a hesitant glance. Then he bent down toward her. "I'm going to step outside for a minute. Don't be afraid. I'll be close by."

With more reluctance than she cared to admit, Rachel let go of his hand. He gave her a quick kiss and then left the room. The door was shut behind him. But as he'd promised, he stood just outside the long window, and she focused on his broad back as the three strangers converged around her.

"How do you feel?" the man Scott had called Girney asked. A woman took hold of Rachel's arm, presumably to assess her pulse rate.

"I'm a little scared."

"Do you know who you are?"

"Yes," she answered, giving him an odd look. "I just don't know who *you* are."

"Do you know *where* you are?"

"I . . . I think—yes, yes, I do."

Something was placed around her upper arm. She looked over at the wide black band, and then it tightened, scaring her so badly that she tried to pull away. The woman beside her assured her that it wouldn't hurt, and asked her to remain still.

"Where are you?" Girney asked, demanding Rachel's attention once again.

"I'm . . . I'm in the future?"

The man nodded, and then pulled out that metal stick with the light on it again. She blinked as he flashed it into her eyes.

"Pulse and blood pressure are within normal ranges," the woman beside her said.

"Pupils look good," Girney replied. "Take a blood sample. Do you feel any pain anywhere?" he asked Rachel.

"No." Something tight was once again wrapped around her arm, and Rachel looked over to see a thick piece of yellowish rope being tied just above her elbow.

"Remain still," the woman said again. "Clench your fist."

The rope was pulling the tiny hairs on her arm, but Rachel did as she was told, hoping that if she cooperated the examination would be over with soon.

The woman turned to the small metal table behind her. "You're going to feel a sharp prick," she said.

"Are you experiencing *anything* unusual?" Girney asked.

Rachel turned to the man and frowned. "Anything *unusual?*" she retorted. "Are you completely serious?" Something not unlike a bee sting stabbed at her arm. "Ouch," she said, and looked to see that the woman had stuck her in the arm with a large, glass syringe. Blood, her own precious blood, was pouring into the small vial attached to it.

"Unclench your fist please." Rachel did as she was told, and the woman finally removed the painful rope. "I'm almost finished," the woman said.

Rachel refocused her eyes on Scott's back through the window. He was still talking with Colonel Tayback, and she felt sure the conversation was about her. She listened carefully, trying to hear what they were saying, but the only sound she heard was the constant low hum of the future.

"What the hell got into your head to bring that woman back here?"

Scott stared at the colonel. "Love," he wanted to say, but he doubted the man would understand that he'd fallen head over heels in just a few short days. "Both our lives were at stake. I didn't have any other choice."

"That's commendable, Captain. But her life could very well still be at stake. Traveling to the future is untested, and considered by some to be totally impossible. Man cannot travel to a nonexistent."

"I couldn't just leave her there to be shot. At least this way she has a fighting chance."

"I hope it's as simple as that," the colonel replied.

Scott turned back to look at Rachel through the window, and their eyes connected through the glass. He loved her. It *was* as simple as *that*. "She looks fine," he stated, hoping he wasn't just trying to convince himself of the fact.

"Let's have the experts decide how fine she is."

The door to the examination room opened, and John Girney stepped out. Scott stared at him, his heart barely beating as he waited for the prognosis. "We're finished," Girney said. "And, by all our estimations at the moment, she's medically sound."

Scott let out a huge sigh and gave John Girney a clap on the shoulder. "That's terrific."

"I suggest, however," Girney added, "that she be watched very closely during the next six hours."

"Why the next six hours?" Scott asked.

"Because that's how long it's gonna take us to charge up the portal and send her back to where the hell she belongs," Tayback replied. He chuckled. "You didn't think you were gonna get to keep her, did ya, Captain?"

To be honest, Scott hadn't been thinking about much of anything except Rachel's safety. But the colonel was right. She wasn't some stray puppy he could bring home and then keep in a box in his closet. She was a human being, with a life of her own to return to.

"So now what?" he asked, not able to keep the note of disappointment from his voice.

The colonel smiled. "Well. You've got six hours, Captain. Why not give the little lady a taste of the twenty-first century?"

Scott leaned back against a tall streetlight in Hangar 23's nearly empty parking lot and watched Rachel take in the sights and sounds around her. She was like a child at Christmas, and he smiled as she spun in a slow circle while staring up at the night sky.

"All these lights are so bright I can barely see the stars," she said in astonishment.

The low roar of a jet taking off across the runway field caught her attention and she squinted at its tiny blinking lights. "*What* is *that*?" she asked.

"An airplane," Scott called to her.

"An airplane," she repeated.

The jet roared, picking up speed, and Scott held out his arms as Rachel quickly moved back against him. Meanwhile the plane moved faster and faster, until it was streaking across the ground in front of them. Rachel watched in silence, her hands covering Scott's, which were folded against her stomach. He felt her flinch when the jet suddenly lurched up into the sky and soared away.

"What kind of bird is an aiplane?" she whispered in awe.

"It's not a bird," he answered, nuzzling her ear. "It's made of metal and a man is inside flying it."

"You're joking," she stated, turning toward him.

"*I* fly them."

She gave him a look of quiet admiration. "*You* know how to make them fly?"

"Don't be too impressed, Rachel," he said, laughing. "I'm only one of about a million people who know how."

"And there are that many airplanes?"

"More."

She smiled brightly up at him, and then glanced around the parking lot. "So, where is this *car* you were telling me about earlier?"

Scott had mentioned the vehicle to her when he'd informed her that he planned to take her to his house. The idea of a horseless carriage had definitely intrigued her. "Right over here."

She ran her fingers along the hood of Pete Averies's Nissan as they walked past it. Scott walked to the center of the parking lot and stopped in front of his black Ford truck. He reached inside the passenger side wheel-well for his lockbox, and then took out his spare key. Rachel watched all this with a quiet fascination, even as he unlocked and opened the car door for her.

The cab light flickered on. But it didn't startle her as he'd expected it to. She was now past the point of being afraid, and was simply curious. "A surprise around every turn," she mumbled, craning her neck to stare up at the cab light.

He moved around the door and stepped up beside

her as she continued to examine the inside of the truck. "Would you like some help climbing in?"

She turned and frowned at him. "You want me to get in this metal box?"

"That's the idea. It's a long way to the house, and I'd rather not walk."

"And this thing will take us there? Without a horse—or even an ox?"

"I'm fresh out of oxen," he said, smiling. He took her around the waist and lifted her, setting her sideways in the bucket seat.

"It's not dangerous, is it?" she asked, frowning as he reached for her shoulder harness and buckled her in.

"Not at all."

"Then what's this thing for?" she asked, tugging at the black belt now strapped across her chest.

"It's just a precaution. I promise I'll be a good boy and not try two-wheeling any corners."

She arched a brow at his smile as he closed her door and then circled around to the driver's side of the truck. "Is there something I'm supposed to hold on to?" she asked as he opened his door and slid behind the wheel.

Your dear life? he was tempted to say. But he didn't, figuring this probably wasn't the best time to tease her. "Just sit back and let me do the driving."

He put the key in the ignition and turned the engine over. Rachel grimaced and pressed back into her seat. "Is everything in the twenty-first century so noisy?"

Scott thought a moment, and then nodded. "Pretty much." He put his foot on the gas pedal and slowly pulled forward.

Rachel took a firm grip on the seat beneath her. "I'm not so sure about this."

"It's okay." Scott paused at the entrance to the street and then slowly pulled out of the parking lot.

"Oh, my goodness," Rachel said as the speedometer began to nudge toward twenty miles an hour. "Shouldn't we . . . shouldn't we slow down a little?"

Scott reached over and took hold of her white-knuckled hand. "Cars are supposed to go fast, Rachel. That's why they're so popular."

She looked out the side window at the car coming up on their right, and seemed to relax now that she saw there were other cars on the street. Scott turned onto the exit ramp toward the freeway and pressed down on the accelerator. The truck lurched, Rachel screamed, and he got four sharp fingernails into the back of his hand.

"It's okay!" he shouted. "Rachel, please don't worry. Everybody's going this fast. It's perfectly normal."

"That only means you're *all* crazy!"

"You're safe," Scott reiterated. Then he laughed. "Christ, you're worse than my grandmother in a car—and she normally won't open her eyes."

"She sounds like a very intelligent woman," Rachel remarked, still bracing herself against the back of the seat. "When is this thing going to stop?"

"The house is twenty-five miles away."

"Twenty-five *miles?*" she repeated, giving him an incredulous look.

"We're going over sixty miles an hour. It'll take us less than thirty minutes to get there." She didn't respond, and he looked over to find her with her nose pressed against the passenger window, staring out over the lit-up city of Seattle. "How are you feeling?"

"Fine. What are all those lights?" she asked breathlessly.

"Homes. Businesses. Streetlights like the ones here alongside the road."

"It looks like we're soaring through a sky full of stars."

Scott smiled and decided she was right. He'd never look at the night lights the same way again.

"So, you're not a pirate, Scott Ramsey," she said, keeping her eyes directed out the window. "You're not a spy. You really are a time-traveler."

"We've just now discovered the technology. The trips I've been making are the first ever attempted."

"Then you make a habit out of involving yourself in other people's lives?"

He gave her a sideways glance, and was relieved to see that she was smiling at him. "Normally I'm only supposed to stay long enough to run some quick tests. Six hours at the most."

"And what happened that kept you for three days?"

"You," he said, flashing her a grin. "And a slight malfunction."

"Then you didn't *choose* to stay?"

"Not at first. But then I was determined not to leave until I knew you were safe."

She was quiet for a moment. "So then if I chose to," she finally said, "I could stay."

Scott gave her a startled look, and she turned to stare back out the passenger window. The idea—no, the meagerest hope that she might choose to remain in the future with him had crossed his mind, but he'd decided not to mention it to her. It wouldn't have been fair to ask her to leave her life and her family behind for him. But knowing she was actually considering the idea made his pulse race. To be able to live and love with this incredible woman for the rest of his life was more than he dared to hope for.

20

"*What'll it be?*"

Rachel leaned forward in her seat and stared at the huge white face that had just spoken to Scott. It was clearly made of some kind of stone, and had a rather odd, large screen mouth. Its hair was orange, sticking straight up on the top and straight out at the sides. It had blue painted eyes, and fat red lips, and it had remarkable vocal abilities.

"Give me a bag of burgers with extra pickles, three large fries, and three Cokes." The large head repeated what Scott had said, and then asked if Scott would like any dessert. "No, thanks," Scott said, and sat back in his seat. He looked over at Rachel and smiled. "I promised my grandmother burgers for dinner the day I left, and I'll never hear the end of it if I don't bring some home now."

"Burgers?"

"Hamburgers. Meat between two rolls. She's got a real thing for them."

"That'll be ten dollars and thirty-five cents," the white head said. "Please pull forward."

Scott made the car move forward around the building and then stop at a small window. Rachel craned her neck again, expecting to see another large head—or maybe a set of large white hands giving Scott his food. But there was a normal-looking young woman standing there holding out her normal-looking hand for Scott's money. "Would you like ketchup?" the young woman asked.

"No thanks."

She handed Scott two white paper bags, and Scott set them in between the two seats. Then he rolled up his window and drove away. Rachel was still staring at the two white bags as the car moved faster down the road. Finally she looked up at Scott. "You get your food from ladies standing in tiny windows?"

"Only on the nights when I don't feel like going home and making something myself."

She sat back. "So that lady makes it for you?"

"And about a hundred thousand other people. It's like a restaurant, only I can take the food home and eat it."

"Oh," she said, smiling. "That's very convenient."

"Yes. We all think so."

He slowed down the car and turned onto another street. He drove slower, and Rachel stared at all the houses they passed. Another few turns, and they pulled up into a drive. Rachel was relieved when Scott turned off the car, took up the two bags of food, opened his door, and got out. Her fingers were practically numb from gripping the seat beneath her.

He came around and opened her door, and helped her down with his free hand. "There," he said. "That wasn't so bad."

"Maybe from your point of view," she remarked.

She'd seen her life flash before her eyes at least five times during the past thirty minutes.

He put his arm around her, pulling her close, and she looked up into his handsome face. The bright lights from the houses surrounding them lit up his eyes and made her press closer to him. "Can I have a kiss before we go inside?"

She smiled. "I might be able to manage that." She stood on tiptoe and pressed her parted lips to his, sinking into the warmth of his embrace. The date may have changed, but the way he could make her feel—the way she felt about him—hadn't changed at all.

He nibbled at her lips for a moment, and then stepped back. "You taste pretty sweet for a one-hundred-and-sixty-year-old woman."

She laughed and smacked him on the chest. "Watch it, Ramsey."

He took her by the hand and led her up the walk toward the porch. A bright light was glowing by the front door as they climbed the three steps toward it.

"Well, I certainly hope those are for me."

Both Rachel and Scott faltered by the door and Rachel turned to see a tiny old woman sitting on a bench to her right. "I haven't eaten in almost four days, you know," the woman added. "I was about to start considering which cat to carve up first."

"There's no choice, Grandma," Scott replied, slipping his arm over Rachel's shoulders. "Rowdy's been askin' for it for months."

The woman stood, with more agility than Rachel would have expected, and walked toward them. "Who's this you've brought home with you?"

"Heloise Ramsey, this is Rachel Warren. Rachel, this is my indomitable grandmother."

"Pleased to meet you," Rachel said.

The woman broke into a bright, toothy smile. "Well, bring her into the house before she freezes to death."

"Grandma, it's sixty-five degrees out here."

The woman moved beneath the porch light and Rachel saw that she was wearing a long unfitted dress and a shawl draped over her shoulders. She had short, curly white hair, and bright brown eyes, and she gave Scott a swat on the arm as she brushed past him. "Bring her in anyway," she retorted.

Scott laughed and followed her into the house, allowing Rachel to step through the doorway ahead of him. "What are you doing sitting there in the *cold,* anyway?"

"Rather freeze to death than starve," the woman replied. Scott shut the front door behind him, and Rachel stepped into the front room. She was immediately charmed by the warm cozy atmosphere. There was a soft, plush brown rug running from wall to wall, a comfortable tan chair to sit in to her left, and a tan leather sofa along the wall in front of her. A tall brass lamp was sitting on a table beside the sofa, and Heloise Ramsey reached out to it. Like magic, the lamp turned on at her touch, brightening the doorway where Rachel was standing.

Rachel felt something brush against her legs, and looked down to see a large white cat curling itself around her ankles. Scott bent down and scratched the cat behind the ears, then walked into the front room and set the bags of food down on the large wooden table.

"There's plenty of food in the house, Grandma," he said. "You wouldn't have starved if I'd stayed away for a month."

"It's all in cans," the woman replied. "You know how much I hate can openers."

"A revulsion you've acquired in just the past few weeks. Sometimes I think you're intentionally trying to drive me nuts."

"Now why would I do a thing like that," the woman said, winking at Rachel. "Come and sit at the table, my dear, and tell me how you came to be in the company of this scamp."

Rachel walked forward, carefully so as not to step on the cat still at her feet, and took a seat at the table. Scott took some of the paper-wrapped food out of the bag and set it down in front of his grandmother, then set some in front of Rachel. Rachel unwrapped it, and smelled its wonderful aroma.

She watched Scott's grandmother pick up her food with her fingers, take a bite, chew, and swallow. "Aren't you going to eat, my dear?" the woman asked.

Rachel hesitated. "What . . . what is it?" she asked softly.

"What is it?" his grandmother repeated, eyeing her carefully. "It's a cheeseburger. You need to get this girl out more often, Scotty."

"Go ahead, Rachel. Try it," Scott urged.

She took a careful bite, chewed, and found she really liked the taste. "It's wonderful," she said with a mouthful of food, and then smiled in embarrassment.

"Give the girl some fries," the old woman commanded.

Scott handed Rachel a small open box with golden spears inside, and Rachel picked one up and placed it in her mouth. She smiled as Scott's grandmother nodded across from her. "The best in town," the woman said. "So tell me," she added. "Is this lovely young lady what's kept you away for the past four days?"

"You might say that," Scott replied, taking the seat at the head of the table.

"And where, exactly, is she from?"

Rachel gave Scott a hesitant look, hoping he wouldn't tell his grandmother the truth. She liked Heloise Ramsey, and didn't want the woman thinking her grandson was courting a lunatic.

"She's not from around here."

"Well, I'd already gathered that, Scott, what with the fear of cheeseburgers and all. Can I assume that this is a serious thing between you two, considering you've brought her home? He never brings women home," she said to Rachel. "I was beginning to doubt he even liked girls."

"Grandma," Scott said in a warning tone, but his lips were twitching as he tried not to smile.

"You can't blame me for being worried," his grandmother replied. She reached over and patted Rachel's hand. "But now I know you won't be alone when my tired old body gives out."

Rachel stopped chewing to angle a glance at Scott. She wanted to reassure him that he would *never* be alone, but she wasn't exactly sure he wanted her to stay with him. He certainly hadn't jumped at the chance to ask her when she'd mentioned it earlier.

"Well, listen," his grandmother said, standing up from the table. "It's nearly eight o'clock. I'm going to head on into my bedroom and watch a little television before I drift off to dreamland."

"Television?" Rachel said without thinking.

The woman gave her a baffled stare, then her eyes narrowed perceptively. "You keep an eye on her, Scotty. Make sure she doesn't stick her fingers in any light sockets."

"Good night, Grandma," Scott stated.

"Good night, Rachel," the woman said, ignoring her grandson's tone. "I certainly hope to see you in the morning."

Rachel smiled after the woman as she left the room and headed down a short hallway. "I like her," Rachel said as a door closed somewhere in the house.

"She speaks her mind, that's for damn sure. Here, have a drink."

"More soda water?" she asked, reaching for the odd cup made out of a heavy type of paper. At that moment a loud noise from across the room startled her and she ended up hitting the cup with her hand and knocking the sticky contents all down the front of her clothes.

She turned to see a large black box coming to life in the far corner. "Good God," she whispered.

"*That's* a television," Scott replied. He stood up, reached for a long, black object on the table in front of the sofa, and the big black box turned off just as magically as it had turned on. "My grandmother has the timer set for eight o'clock just in case she falls asleep before prime time."

He came back to Rachel and picked up some folded papers on the table, intending to use them to clean the mess off her clothes. He stared at the front of her shirt. "This isn't going to work. I think you're going to need to change. Maybe take a shower."

"A shower?"

He gave her a surprised look and then broke into a steady smile. "Come along, Miss Warren. Allow me to introduce you to the wonders of indoor plumbing."

He stood outside and listened to her flush the toilet five times before she finally told him he could come in. When Scott stepped into the bathroom, Rachel was standing there in nothing but a big, fluffy, white towel. He decided, then and there, that she wouldn't be taking this shower alone.

He walked toward the shower stall and turned on the water. She came forward and watched over his shoulder as he adjusted the temperature. Then she reached out and stuck her hand in the spray to be sure it was what it appeared to be. "I love your world, Scott Ramsey," she said, laughing. "Everything is made so easy!"

He moved up behind her. "Go ahead and get in. I'll show you where the soap and shampoo are in a minute."

She gave him a hesitant glance, and he turned and walked toward the sink so she could have a little privacy. When he heard the door to the shower close, however, the blood started singing in his veins. With determined hands, he began unbuttoning his shirt.

A few moments later, Scott opened the door of the shower and stepped in quietly behind Rachel. She was standing beneath the spray, her eyes closed and her face turned into the water, oblivious to his presence.

He pressed up against her and slipped his hands around her tiny waist, letting her feel his swelling desire. He wasn't sure how Rachel would react to his forward actions, but he was more than pleased when she turned in his arms and started kissing him as though she'd been waiting for this moment her entire life.

He certainly wasn't going to question his luck, either. Within seconds his body was screaming for hers, and he pressed her back against the shower wall, and lifted her legs around his hips. He was inside her instantly, moving within her. The water mingled with her lips as he enjoyed her mouth, and then dampened his tongue as he raised her and kissed her aroused nipples.

Time stood still for them as they loved each other completely and without hesitation. In the end Scott knew what he had to do. He would ask Rachel Ann Warren to marry him, and stay with him forever.

*   *   *

They stayed in the shower until the hot water was gone, and then took a long, leisurely time drying each other off. Scott dug a pair of his grandmother's sweats out of the dryer, and let Rachel borrow one of his Seattle Seahawks sweatshirts. She swam in the shirt, but the sweats hugged her hips just right, and Scott knew he could never let his grandmother wear them again.

He tossed her clothes into the washing machine, and then took Rachel into the kitchen to let her explore. She spent the next two hours playing with everything from the blender to the light switches. Finally he maneuvered her back into the living room, and just when he thought he had a hope of gaining her attention, she opened the coat closet and spotted the vacuum cleaner. The next thing Scott knew Rachel was vacuuming the damn living-room floor like a madwoman. When the carpet was spotless, she put things down to suck up.

Finally he couldn't bear it anymore and put the Hoover back in the closet. Then he pulled Rachel down onto the couch beside him, and tried to work up the courage to ask her the question on his mind.

"What's that over there?" she asked, pointing to the answering machine.

Scott took hold of her hand, and laughed. "I feel like I'm getting thrown over for the appliances."

"Oh," she said, turning a shade of red. "I'm sorry. Everything is just so . . . so *fascinating*. I'm a little overwhelmed."

"And I'm a whole lot overwhelmed by you," he said seriously. "Do you have any idea how hard and how quickly I've fallen in love with you?" Her blush intensified, and she looked down to hide her embarrassment.

He took her by the chin and lifted her face, brushing his thumb across the silkiness of her bottom lip. "Do you have any idea?"

"I think I've . . . experienced something like that myself recently," she admitted, smiling shyly.

Encouraged, he edged closer to her. "Do you like it here?"

"It's wonderful."

"You mentioned in the car that you might choose to stay. And I was . . . I was hoping that I might be able to convin—"

The phone rang, and Scott let out a groan. He would have ignored it, but he knew if he did his grandmother would pick it up in her bedroom and then come out to tell him it was for him anyway. "Hold that thought," he said to her, scrambling across the room to pick up the receiver.

"Hello?"

"Captain?"

Scott straightened. "Yes."

"This is Tayback."

The tone of Colonel Tayback's voice made Scott's muscles tense, and he looked over at Rachel. "Yeah?"

"You've got to bring her back to the lab, Captain. There's been a development."

"What kind of development?"

"I know you care for her, son," the colonel replied. "But she's got to go back. Otherwise she's not gonna last out the night."

21

The first thing Scott noticed when he charged into the lab with Rachel was the roar of the coolers. They'd already initiated the portal.

Colonel Tayback and John Girney met them at the door. "Tell me what's going on," Scott demanded.

"She's demolecularizing."

"In English, goddamn it!" Scott shouted.

"Captain," Tayback said calmly. "It's just as we've suspected. A human being cannot travel to a nonexistent. This little lady is literally beginning to fall apart at the seams."

Scott looked down into Rachel's frightened face. "How do you feel?"

"Fine. I feel fine."

"Any headache?" Girney asked, stooping down to look into her eyes.

"No," Rachel replied.

"What about dizziness?"

"Well, yes. But Scott said that was normal after coming through the portal."

Scott's heart thudded. "The dizziness only lasts a few minutes, Rachel."

"Anything else?" Girney asked, flashing his penlight in her eyes. "How's your eyesight?"

"A little . . . blurry. But I'm sure that's just because of all the bright lights."

"Her pupils are sluggish," Girney said.

"Look at this, Captain," the colonel said. He held up a vial of red liquid. "This is the blood sample they took from her a few hours ago."

Scott stared at the thin red liquid, and his mouth went dry. He slipped his arm around Rachel's back and pulled her closer to him. "What can we do?" he asked hoarsely.

"We can send her back where she belongs," John Girney replied.

"No!" Rachel cried. She looked up into Scott's face and the tears shining in her eyes squeezed at his heart. "I want to stay here! I *choose* to stay here with you!"

Scott stared down into her beautiful face and wondered how in the world he was ever going to live without her. "Will her body chemistry return to normal if we return her to her own time?"

"What are you saying?" Rachel whispered.

"We have every reason to believe it will."

"And if she stays here? Is there anything we can do to stabilize her?"

"Nothing. She'll begin hemorrhaging within the hour."

"Open"—a sob caught in Scott's throat—"Open the chamber door."

"No!" Rachel cried, throwing herself against his chest. "I won't leave you! I *can't* leave you!"

"You have to, Rachel," he whispered to her. "You'll die if you don't go back."

He tried to lead her toward the transportation chamber, but she dragged her feet. So he swept her up into his arms and carried her there. She buried her face against his neck and sobbed.

Loving her had been the easiest thing he'd ever done. Letting her go would be the hardest.

Rachel swore to herself she wouldn't cry any more. They'd had four brief glorious days together, and she wouldn't let him remember her as a weepy mass at his feet. Still, she had to bite her bottom lip to keep her chin from trembling as Scott held her close for one last good-bye.

"They're sending you as close to your hometown as possible," he said against her ear so she could hear him over the roar of what he called "the coolers." There was a lot of emotion in his choked voice, and her own chest tightened painfully. "You'll have a few moments of disorientation once you reach your destination. . . . Remember to sit down and let your head clear."

He took her by the shoulders and pressed her away from him. Rachel reached out and ran her fingers over his face, memorizing his features one last time. He mouthed the words "I love you," and she broke her promise to herself as tears began to dribble down her cheeks.

She kissed him then, closing her mouth over his in a bittersweet caress that blended the salt of both their tears. They'd loved for such a short time, never knowing that the memories would have to last them a lifetime.

Finally, she pulled away and turned without looking at him, knowing it would break her heart if she saw her own anguish mirrored in his eyes. She swallowed hard, and began walking into the light. "I'll love you forever,

Rachel Ann Warren!" she heard him call to her. "Till the end of time."

Before she could give in to the urge to run back into his arms, Rachel lunged forward into the light. There was a strong pull at her body. A moment of nothingness.

And then she was scattered like dust in the wind, and returned to 1862. But she had left her heart and soul behind.

Scott didn't go home until almost six o'clock the next morning. He arrived with an empty tank of gas and a very large bottle of Irish whiskey. His grandmother was sitting on the couch when he walked in the front door.

"Are you drunk?" was the first thing she asked him.

"No. But I damn sure plan to be."

"Where's Rachel?" the woman demanded. "Did you two have a fight?"

He felt new tears choking him. "She couldn't stay," he replied, dropping down into the lounge chair.

"Then where did she go?"

"She went home, Grandma." He let go with a bitter laugh. "You might say love wasn't strong enough to save her."

"Then I was right. You do love her."

"Without a doubt," he muttered.

"Then why didn't you go with her?"

Scott shook his head. "You don't understand. She lives so far away that if I went with her I wouldn't be coming back."

"Ever?"

"No."

"Do you hate the nineteenth century that much then?" He blinked at her in surprise, and she smirked at him. "You know better than anyone I'm not a stupid old woman, Scott Ramsey. I hear what you and your friends from the project talk about during the poker games you hold here once a month. It wasn't hard for me to tell that that young woman wasn't exactly modern."

Scott shook his head. He should have known better than to think he could pull one over on her.

"Why didn't you go with her?" she demanded.

"Because I have other obligations."

"Me, you mean."

He nodded, giving her a steady look.

"So, you've given up the love of your life just to sit here and babysit me? And here I thought you'd inherited the brains in the family."

"I promised Grandpa—"

"And if he were here right now, he'd be the first one to smack you on the back of your head! I made a decision while you were gone, Scotty. I've decided that I am moving in with Patricia Hollenbeck—"

"Grandma—"

"And I won't listen to a word you have to say about it. I plan to spend my final years playing shuffleboard and gawking at old men's fannies, not watching you waste away your life. And, in my opinion, that's exactly what you're going to be doing if you don't go after that girl."

"You'd want to spend your final years *alone*?" he asked incredulously.

"*I* won't be alone. I've lived a full life. Loved a man deeply, and had a beautiful son who gave me a beautiful grandson. I have friends, and dozens of wonderful memories to keep me company. You, Scott. You are the one who will be alone."

Scott closed his eyes, and fought the tightening in his chest.

"Follow your heart," his grandmother advised him. "Before it's too late."

She stood from the couch and went into her bedroom, leaving Scott to contemplate all she'd said. She was releasing him from his promise, telling him—no commanding him to go and make a life for himself with the woman he loved.

The doorbell rang and he stood from the chair. He opened the door to find a tall blond man he didn't recognize standing in the bright morning sunlight. "I'm not interested," Scott said, and tried to close the door.

"Oh, I'm not selling."

Scott frowned at the man, not recognizing him as any of his neighbors. "Then what do you want?"

"I'm, uh, I'm from Cleveland. This is going to sound really strange to you, sir, I know, but I've just flown eight hours to get here, and I wasn't even sure what I'd find. Please, may I come in?"

Scott sighed and stepped aside. "Yeah, sure. Why not."

"Thank you," the man said, stepping past Scott and into the house. "I'm here to ask you a few questions about a relative of mine." He turned and held out a small, ragged book. "I was hoping whoever lived here could shed some light on this?"

Scott stared down at the book, not recognizing it. "What is it?"

"My wife and I were going through an old trunk of things left to me by my grandmother, and we found this. It's my great-great-great-grandmother's diary."

"Uh-huh."

"Well, there's an address"—the man carefully cracked the old book open to a page halfway to the back—"here. Isn't that *this* address?"

Scott stared at the smeared black ink. It was true. His address was clearly printed in neat handwriting, along with the date, May 20, 2001.

"It's kind of strange, don't you think?" the man said. "Your address and today's date in a diary dating back almost one hundred and forty years."

Scott's heart began to pound. He took the book from the man and looked further down the page. *My darling Scott,* it read. *It's been nearly six hours since—*

He flipped the page but there was nothing else written. Nothing else in the entire diary.

"I know," the man said. "Something pretty important must have interrupted Grandma Rachel. I thought . . . well, that is to say . . . I was hoping that whoever lived here might have an explanation for this?"

Scott took a moment to run his fingers over the fragile page in the diary. It was clear that Rachel had been writing to him. And it was also clear, by the very existence of this man, that she had married and had children. She'd gone on with her life. Just as he should do now. He needed to let her go.

He carefully closed the book. "It must be just a coincidence."

"*Coincidence?*"

He handed the book back to the man. "What other reasonable theory could there be?"

"I was hoping you'd have more to tell me than that—"

"Like maybe I knew the woman in another life?" Scott replied, hoping his smile didn't appear too bitter.

The man laughed, looking a little embarrassed. "Of course not. Frankly, I don't know what I was hoping. It's been a mystery for so long. . . ." Finally he shrugged. "Well . . . you can't blame a man for trying. I'm sorry I bothered you." He turned and headed for the door.

"Your Grandma Rachel," Scott called after him. "Did she live a long, happy life?"

The man paused on the threshold and smiled back at him. "She married and moved out west to California where she and her husband struck it rich investing in the railroads."

Jealousy, hot and thick, dug at Scott's heart. "Sounds like she married a wise man."

"Yeah. I hear Grandpa Scott was ahead of his time."

Scott froze. "Grandpa *Scott*?"

"That was his name. Scott Jacob Ramsey."

Scott felt as if a cannonball had just slammed into his stomach, and he stood rooted to the floor even after the man had left, a myriad of thoughts spinning around in his head. And then he heard his grandmother come into the room behind him. "Well, Scott Jacob Ramsey? Your grandmother seems to carry little weight around here, but are you gonna listen to your great-great-great-grandson?"

And in that moment Scott knew. He and Rachel were meant to be together.

He ran across the room and planted a smacking kiss on his grandmother's forehead. "You are a wonderful old woman!"

"'Bout time you figured that out."

Laughing, Scott hurried to the phone and dialed with shaking fingers. It rang and rang, until finally he heard the clink of someone picking up the receiver on the other end.

"Hello?" a groggy voice said.

"Pete?"

"Yeah . . . Scott? Is that you?"

"Do you know how to initiate Stargazer?"

"What? Why?"

"Do you!"

"Yeah. Yeah. It's a pretty basic command."

"Meet me at the lab."

"What are you planning?"

"Pete, you know all that gratitude you guys have all been feeling toward me for risking my life on this project?"

"Yeah," Pete said warily.

"Well, Pete, old buddy. It's payback time."

Epilogue

Just as she'd been promised, Rachel had been transported to a field just outside of Sleepy Bluff, Ohio. And it was only six hours from the time she and Scott had disappeared by the river.

When she'd walked into the front yard her parents had come charging out to greet her. Startled by her sudden arrival, they'd assailed her with questions. And Rachel had burst into tears. Her mother had had to help her off to her room. Rachel hadn't known what to say to either of them, and so she'd spent the night crying until she'd had no more tears left.

Now she was sitting alone on the front porch, her diary in her lap, trying to come up with a way to put the last five days of her life into words.

She rocked gently in the old rocking chair that her mother used to cuddle her in when she was little, and lifted her tear-filled eyes to the wind, hoping it might sweep away some of her heartache. But the kind of anguish she was feeling couldn't disappear with a simple breeze. She wasn't even sure time could heal this wound cut so deeply into her soul.

She lowered her eyes to the diary in her hands. She'd been writing in it off and on for the past two years, jotting down her experiences and her dreams. All childish and inconsequential until now.

Finally she cracked it open to the last entry, dated just before she'd left for Georgia, and turned to the next page. She reached down and dabbed her quill pen into the inkwell sitting on the porch beside her chair, and jotted down the last date she'd seen Scott, his house number, his street, and the name of his city. Somehow maybe her diary would reach him someday.

Then she took a deep breath and began a new line a few spaces down.

My darling Scott, she wrote. *It's been nearly six hours since—*

And then a sound a few feet away caught her attention. She looked up and could barely believe her eyes.

"My darling Scott," he said, coming toward her. "It's been nearly six hours. Six hours because that's how long it took to fire up that goddamn time-portal again."

With a strangled cry, Rachel flew out of the rocking chair and into Scott's strong arms. "Oh, my God!" she cried. "You came back! You came back!"

"I couldn't live without you, Rachel," he whispered, and kissed her long and deep.

Rachel ran her hands over his back and shoulders, praying she wasn't dreaming, and then she pulled away suddenly. "Swear to me you'll never leave again!" she demanded.

"I swear I'll never leave again," he replied intently.

She threw her arms around him again and sobbed. "I love you," she whispered. "I love you!"

"Marry me, Rachel," he said softly. She pulled back again and stared into his warm brown eyes. "Before your brothers find out we lied and beat the living tar out of me," he added with a laugh.

"*I* would have beat the living tar out of you if you hadn't asked," she retorted. New tears filled her eyes as she ran her fingers over his handsome face. "I didn't think I'd ever see you again."

Scott smiled, and gazed down into her beautiful pale green eyes. "Rachel, my love . . . you are always jumping to the wrong conclusions."

Let HarperMonogram Sweep You Away!

Touched by Angels by Debbie Macomber
From the bestselling author of *A Season of Angels* and *The Trouble with Angels*. The much-loved angelic trio—Shirley, Goodness, and Mercy—are spending this Christmas in New York City. And three deserving souls are about to have their wishes granted by this dizzy, though divinely inspired, crew.

Till the End of Time by Suzanne Elizabeth
The latest sizzling time-travel romance from the award-winning author of *Destiny's Embrace*. Scott Ramsey has a taste for adventure and a way with the ladies. When his time-travel experiment transports him back to Civil War Georgia, he meets his match in Rachel Ann Warren, a beautiful Union spy posing as a Southern belle.

A Taste of Honey by Stephanie Mittman
After raising her five siblings, marrying the local minister is a chance for Annie Morrow to get away from the farm. When she loses her heart to widower Noah Eastman, however, Annie must choose between a life of ease and a love no money can buy.

A Delicate Condition by Angie Ray
Golden Heart Winner. A marriage of convenience weds innocent Miranda Rembert to the icy Lord Huntsley. But beneath his lordship's stern exterior, fires of passion linger—along with a burning desire for the marital pleasures only Miranda can provide.

Reckless Destiny by Teresa Southwick
Believing that Arizona Territory is no place for a lady, Captain Kane Carrington sent proper easterner Cady Tanner packing. Now the winsome schoolteacher is back, and ready to teach Captain Carrington a lesson in love.

And in case you missed last month's selections . . .

Liberty Blue by Robin Lee Hatcher
Libby headed west, running from her ruthless father and her privileged life. Remington Walker will do anything to locate her, as long as her father keeps paying him. But when Remington does he realizes she's worth more than money can buy.

Shadows in the Mirror by Roslynn Griffith
Iphigenia Wentworth is determined to find her missing baby in West Texas. She never expected to find love with a local rancher along the way.

Yesterday's Tomorrows by Margaret Lane
Montana rancher Abby De Coux is magically transported back to the year 1875 in order to save her family's ranch. There she meets ruggedly handsome Elan, who will gamble his future to make her his forever.

The Covenant by Modean Moon
From the author of the acclaimed *Evermore*, a spellbinding present-day romance expertly interwoven with a nineteenth-century love story.

Brimstone by Sonia Simone
After being cheated at the gaming tables by seasoned sharper Katie Starr, the Earl of Brynston decides to teach the silly American girl a lesson. But soon the two are caught in a high stakes game in which they both risk losing their hearts.

MAIL TO: HarperCollins Publishers
P.O. Box 588 Dunmore, PA 18512−0588
OR CALL: 1-800-331-3761 (Visa/MasterCard)

YES! Please send me the books I have checked:
- ❏ **TOUCHED BY ANGELS** 108344-5 ....$5.99 U.S./$6.99 CAN.
- ❏ **TILL THE END OF TIME** 108408-5 ....$4.99 U.S./$5.99 CAN.
- ❏ **A TASTE OF HONEY** 108394-1 ....$4.50 U.S./$5.50 CAN.
- ❏ **A DELICATE CONDITION** 108378-X ....$4.50 U.S./$5.50 CAN.
- ❏ **RECKLESS DESTINY** 108370-4 ....$4.99 U.S./$5.99 CAN.
- ❏ **LIBERTY BLUE** 108389-5 ....$5.99 U.S./$6.99 CAN.
- ❏ **SHADOWS IN THE MIRROR** 108355-0 ....$4.99 U.S./$5.99 CAN.
- ❏ **YESTERDAY'S TOMORROWS** 108353-4 ......$4.50 U.S./$5.50 CAN.
- ❏ **THE COVENANT** 108314-3 ....$4.99 U.S./$5.99 CAN.
- ❏ **BRIMSTONE** 108376-3 ....$4.50 U.S./$5.50 CAN.

SUBTOTAL...$_____
POSTAGE & HANDLING.............................$ 2.00
SALES TAX (Add applicable sales tax)..........$_____
TOTAL ....$_____

Name_____

Address_____

City_____ State_____ Zip Code_____

M010

Order 4 or more titles and postage & handling is FREE! Orders of less than 4 books, please include $2.00 p/h. Remit in US funds. Do not send cash. Allow up to 6 weeks for delivery. Prices subject to change. Valid only in U.S. and Canada.

Buy 4 or more and get FREE postage & handling!

Would you travel through time to find your soul mate?

TIME TRAVEL *Romance*

Prairie Knight by Donna Valentino

Juliette Walburn struggled to behave as a prim, practical widow should in the eyes of her homesteading neighbors. Certainly she would never believe that a medieval knight could travel through time to land on her doorstep in Kansas and offer her a love that could surpass the bounds of time.

Once Upon a Pirate by Nancy Block

Zoe Dunham did not expect to spend a vacation aboard a ship engaged in the War of 1812 with a sinfully handsome pirate. Could a beleaguered divorced mother from the twentieth century possibly find love with a nineteenth-century pirate?

In My Dreams by Susan Sizemore

Sammy Bergen was summoned back in time to medieval Ireland by a druidic song—and the singer, the bewitchingly lovely Brianna. Could Sammy and Brianna defy time to find perfect happiness together?

Destined to Love by Suzanne Elizabeth

A guardian angel sent Dr. Josie Reed back to the Wild West of 1881 to tend to a captured outlaw. Though Josie was immediately attracted to Kurtis Mitchell's dangerous good looks, the last thing she wanted was to go on the run with him when he made a daring escape.

*Awarded Best Time Travel Romance of 1994 by *Romantic Times*.

Harper *Monogram*

The Mark of Distinctive Women's Fiction

Echoes and Illusions
by Kathy Lynn Emerson

Lauren Ryder has everything she wants, but then the dreams start—dreams so real she fears she's losing her mind. Something happened to Lauren in the not-so-distant past that she can't remember. As she desperately tries to piece together the missing years of her life, a shocking picture emerges. Who is Lauren Ryder, really?

The Night Orchid by Patricia Simpson

In Seattle Marissa Quinn encounters a doctor conducting ancient Druid time-travel rituals and meets Alek, a glorious pre-Roman warrior trapped in the modern world. Marissa and Alek discover that though two millennia separate their lives, nothing can sever the bond forged between their hearts.

Destiny Awaits by Suzanne Elizabeth

Tess Harper found herself in Kansas in the year 1885, face-to-face with the most captivating, stubborn man she'd ever met—and two precious little girls who needed a mother. Could this man, and this family, be her true destiny?

MAIL TO: **HarperCollins Publishers**
P.O. Box 588 Dunmore, PA 18512-0588
OR CALL: (800) 331-3761 (Visa/MC)
Yes! Please send me the books I have checked:

❏**PRAIRIE KNIGHT** 108282-1 . . . .$4.50 U.S./$5.50 CAN.
❏**ONCE UPON A PIRATE** 108366-6 . . . .$4.50 U.S./$5.50 CAN.
❏**IN MY DREAMS** 108134-5. . . . .$4.99 U.S./$5.99 CAN.
❏**DESTINY AWAITS** 108342-9. . . . .$4.99 U.S./$5.99 CAN.
❏**DESTINED TO LOVE** 108225-2 . . . .$4.99 U.S./$5.99 CAN.
❏**THE NIGHT ORCHID** 108064-0 . . . .$4.99 U.S./$5.99 CAN.
❏**ECHOES AND ILLUSIONS** 108022-5. . . . .$4.99 U.S./$5.99 CAN.

Order 4 or more titles and postage & handling is **FREE!** Orders of less than 4 books, please include $2.00 postage & handling. Remit in US funds. Do not send cash. Allow up to 6 weeks delivery. Prices subject to change. Valid only in US and Canada.

SUBTOTAL . . . .$_____
POSTAGE AND HANDLING . . . .$_____
SALES TAX (Add applicable sales tax) . . . . . .$_____
TOTAL . . . .$_____
Name_____
Address_____
City_____State_____Zip_____

M006

ATTENTION: ORGANIZATIONS AND CORPORATIONS

Most HarperPaperbacks are available at special quantity discounts for bulk purchases for sales promotions, premiums, or fund-raising. For information, please call or write:
Special Markets Department, HarperCollins Publishers,
10 East 53rd Street, New York, N.Y. 10022.
Telephone: (212) 207-7528. Fax: (212) 207-7222.